IRMA

Hurricane Irma

Kerry Costello

Kerry Costello Books

CONTENTS

CHAPTER 1

BEFORE

Hurricane Irma
September 2017
Naples Florida

Naples wasn't forecast to be directly in Irma's path, so they ignored the advice to get out. Then on Saturday, things changed, and Naples was now projected to be directly in the Hurricane's path. They watched and listened to the continuous news updates on the progress of the hurricane. At midday, despite the high winds, Sean told his teenage son and daughter to go out in the garden and get some fresh air while they still could.

Not knowing how long the hurricane would last, Sarah stocked up with food, bottled water and other supplies. Sean already had a standby generator, so he made sure he had enough gas and prepared the transfer switch to ensure they had power if the main supply failed. They went to bed on Saturday night confident they were adequately prepared for any eventuality.

By late Sunday morning, the storm finally arrived in earnest and over the next couple of hours, slowly but surely, built in strength. The winds became relentless, growing in intensity. After an hour or so the storm seemed to abate. Sean turned away from the window, looked at his family sitting huddled on the couch, and gave them a reassuring 'told you so' smile. Then the wind increased again and became ferocious. The house took a battering, it shook as the wind slammed into it. They heard a loud creaking, then a ripping noise as part of the roof was suddenly torn off. A howling wind blasted through the house. Sean gasped, Elisabeth screamed. Michael yelled and Sarah put her arms around each child pulling them close. They stayed like that for a short while, then Sarah withdrew her arms, crossed herself, bowed her head and put her hands together in prayer. The children looked at her, then followed suit.

The hurricane was reaching its zenith, the wind screaming. The building shook again under the onslaught of the hurricane's power. Sean had never heard a noise like it. He told friends later, he imagined it was like standing next to a jumbo jet's engines revving at full power. Massive gusts of wind pulverized the house and as Sarah watched through the gap in the window boards, a palm tree was ripped out of the ground by the sheer force of the wind and thrown on to the power lines that fed electricity to their home.

The circuit breaker box exploded, and the lights went out.

Sean found his flashlight, scurried to the generator, switched it on and threw the transfer switch. The lights and power came back on. Now, as the vicious winds continued to rip, Sean got scared. The storm then became impossibly louder and even more intense, buffeting the house relentlessly as if it were angry at them for staying. Sean looked at his cell. No bars. He figured the cell towers had gone down. They were well and truly on their own.

He went cautiously through the house to assess what damage had been done to the roof. Fortunately, the roof had held, but water had poured in through the gaping hole in the ceiling and pooled on the floor. The wind shrieked again, and Sean wondered how long it would be before the entire building was torn apart. He'd lived through Hurricane Wilma but never experienced anything like this. Closing his eyes, he also started to pray.

Some ten minutes later, as if in answer to his prayers, the winds started to die down, slowly at first. Sean held his breath, then gradually the wind began to fade. He breathed more easily. Apart from a few strong gusts, the storm now seemed to have blown itself out. By the evening, the wind had lost its destructive power and they all felt able to go to their beds and get some well needed sleep. The mess would have to wait.

Hurricane Irma had made landfall over the Florida Keys the morning of Sept. 10, 2017, as a category four hurricane. By then, it had already caused massive damage and at least 134 deaths on its journey to mainland USA from its origins in the Cape Verde Islands. It had carved a path of devastation across the Caribbean. At its peak, Irma was a Category five hurricane with wind speeds of 177 mph. Six million Florida residents evacuated coastal areas as it headed for south Florida.

At the time, Frankie Armstrong was back home in the UK living happily with his wife Penny. He'd recently returned from a trip to southwest Florida, paying back a favor to a US soldier who saved his life during the Gulf War in 2003. Frankie loved Naples and was concerned at the damage the hurricane might do to the area. He'd stayed in regular contact with his friends there, who were thankfully relatively unscathed by the event.

***

What Frankie couldn't possibly know at that time, was just how much Hurricane Irma, a dramatic but remote event, would impact his own life in the not-too-distant future. He wasn't alone in this. There were other individuals anxiously watching that day, individuals whose future lives would intertwine with Frankie's and be severely impacted by the aftermath of Irma. She was destructive enough at the time, but for certain individuals, the aftermath of Irma would be worse and much more destructive…

CHAPTER 2

BEFORE

Sunday 10 September 2017
Virginia Water England

Brandon sat in the living room of his elegant mini mansion anxiously watching CNN live. The reporters were broadcasting from the balcony of the Inn on Fifth in Naples. Brandon Mellor was in good shape and normally looked ten years younger than his actual age, but tonight, looked much older. Anguish etched on his face, clutching his glass of scotch as he listened to the reporters describing the scenes of devastation in various parts of the city.

He watched and listened intently as CNN reporter Chris Cuomo leaned into the wind, struggling to make himself heard. Rain sheeting down on the hotel balcony he was broadcasting from.

'This is the real deal,' Cuomo shouted into the mic. 'Branches coming off trees, water flooding the rain lashed streets and inundating shop premises.' His on-going commentary punctuated with clips of violent destruction in various parts of Naples. Then came the information Brandon had been dreading. Cuomo, holding his hand to his ear to emphasize the strength of the howling wind, looked straight into the camera lens, a grim expression on his face and said,

'It's just been predicted there'll be a fifteen-foot sea surge minimum, on Naples shores. Lord alone knows what that damage that will wreak on boats and shoreline properties.?'

Brandon put his head in his hands and moaned. His condo sat on the edge of Venetian Bay which was tidal and would act in concert with any sea surge.

"Oh dear," said his wife Fiona, who'd just walked into the room, cup of tea in hand. She was what people would describe as willowy, had classic features, natural blondish, hair and a slightly haughty air about her.

"Won't that do some damage to our condo darling? I mean, how high does this surge have to be to flood our place?" Brandon replied.

"A fifteen-foot surge, or anything near to that, will crash through into our condo and utterly destroy everything inside."

"Oh well, never mind Brandon."

"Never mind!" Brandon exclaimed, "never fucking mind!?" he shouted.

"Now now, no need for coarse language dear. I meant never mind because we're well insured, aren't we?"

"No, I don't think so, not against flood damage, but it's not just that."

"Then what is it, Brandon? I mean, its only furniture and stuff. We can afford to replace everything, can't we? I hardly ever go there so it's not a problem for me, but I know you adore the place. Call one of your friends there and find out what's really happening. You know how these news people like to exaggerate. I never believe anything they say"

"No one there Fi. They all left a couple of days ago. They were told to leave. Most of the Snowbirds have gone back up north, the rest have gone to stay with relations in other parts of the country until this is over. I need to get out there."

"Are you mad Brandon, you can't go out there now. Anyway, the planes won't be flying. Just have another drink and forget about it. Things will look much better in the morning, they always do."

Brandon shook his head and moaned again. *If only you knew*, he thought.

CHAPTER 3

Sean Kennedy

Sean Michael Kennedy had been born into hard working second generation Irish Catholic family in Fort Myers. Being the middle one of three siblings, he felt a little neglected at times. His father was a builder, a bricklayer. His mother a seamstress. He learnt the ten commandments at his mother's knee and took them to all to heart, with the exception of number eight, *Thou shalt not steal.* His habit of thieving developed in early childhood. At first it was just a case of taking toys from his brothers, hiding them, then feigning innocence when they were invariably found by his mother.

His mother put it down to childhood sibling envy and tried to compensate, but the damage was done. Sean felt he was treated less fairly than his sister and brother. Eventually his stealing became a problem and his father decided he needed a teaching lesson. This involved a leather belt and confinement to his room. Unsurprisingly, this had the reverse effect to that intended and made matters worse. But Sean wasn't stupid and not wishing to receive any more punishment, pretended he was a reformed character. And for a while he was.

As he grew up, Sean realized people were too trusting and stealing was quite easy. It was not getting caught that was the difficult bit. But he was a bright enough boy and quickly learned how to hide stuff and play the innocent. On leaving school his father got him a job with a friend and Sean learnt the building trade. As soon as he was confident of his skills as a builder come handyman, he left his then employer and went free-lance as it were. This gave Sean the opportunity to enter lots of homes and various premises where he could make assessments of goods worth stealing and note any security vulnerabilities.

Sean was also smart enough to realize that the cops would soon be able to link robberies with his attendance at these places, if thefts always occurred while he'd been there, or shortly afterwards. So, he always waited a reasonable length of time before going back to take whatever it was he'd found. Often, if the job seemed a bit too large or risky for him to feel comfortable doing, he'd sell the information on to another thief, then provide himself with rock solid alibi for when the robbery was carried out.

Sean had never been caught, ever. The lesson taught in his early days by his heavy-handed father, had served him well in that regard. Sean was a charmer and typically Irish, had the gift of the gab and an open smiley face. He was his mother's favorite and could make her laugh. When caught doing something wrong as a child, Sean would plead with his mother not to tell his father. She almost never did, but instead would scold him unconvincingly and always finished his telling off by saying he must have kissed the blarney stone at least twice.

His combined earnings from his honest work and his less than honest activities meant that Sean could get married and buy a modest single-family home in Naples by the time he was twenty-four years old. And so, Sean and Sarah had two children of their own and he settled into married life, reasonably content with his lot. That was until Hurricane Irma came along and changed all that for good.

Sean got the call on Tuesday evening, two days after the hurricane had passed through Naples, nearly wrecking his house and terrifying his family. He'd been busy repairing the roof, getting soaking wet as heavy rain continued to fall. Sean hated heights and hated getting wet. His wife Sarah and the children had mopped up the mess the inundation of water had caused in the house Carpets and furniture had been hauled outside in the hope of them drying out in the Florida sunshine, but as the rain never let up, there was never a chance of them getting dry now, most of the items were ruined.

Sean's phone trilled. He turned and sat up on the roof, feet anchored in the gutter. Retrieving the phone from his jacket pocket, he looked and recognized the number as one of his sometime contractors. Sean smiled, knowing at least there'd be plenty of well-paid work repairing the massive damage caused by Irma. His services would be sought after by anyone he knew, and he'd be able to charge a huge premium on his normal rates. *Maybe some other rich pickings as well?* He tried to calculate what he could get away with charging for his services in the current situation. *Always a silver lining* he thought as he answered his cell.

"Hi Alan, how ya doin'?"

"Busy as a dam full of beavers. Listen Sean, I got some jobs you might be interested in. All urgent as you might have guessed, so the pay's good."

"Well, I'm supposed to be working on a house on Crayton next week."

"So, you sayin' you're not available?"

"No man I'm not saying that. I think the Crayton people are on vacation for a while. If I can't to them before they get back, I'll just get Sarah to call 'em and tell say I'll be delayed for a while. I'm sure it won't be a problem. Okay, so I got a choice, do I?"

"Well, I guess you do. You want outdoor or indoor?"

"Hmm," said Sean, "depends, can you run me through the options. Don't bother with roof work, I ain't interested. I'm having to fix my own roof right now, in this weather! Hurricane blew a hole in it. Any inside work? I kinda like the idea of inside at the moment."

"Yeah, sure," said Alan and ran through a brief description of jobs on his list. Sean assessed them as he went through the ones on offer. One piqued his interest. *Some rich pickings maybe?*

"Alan, go back to the condo job. Ten first floor condos to strip out you said?"

"Yeah, flooding then mold. Roman Plaza on Harbour Drive. They got to move quickly. All the owners moved out already, some weren't there when it happened. Out of towners. Either hadn't come down yet or fled the hurricane, whatever. So, the condo management made the decision to rip out everything, furniture, carpets, walls, kitchens, you name it, it all has to go."

"So, big insurance job? Wow, put me down for that," said Sean, mentally rubbing his hands with glee at the prospect of what the absent owners may have left for him to plunder.

"When can you start? I need men on this yesterday."

"I'll be there at seven sharp tomorrow, okay?" said Sean.

"Great," said Alan. "Look I know there's the temptation to take stuff if it's being dumped anyway but be careful. Insurance inspectors and assessors want to see evidence, don't forget that. Stuff goes missing, won't look good on me, okay?"

"Don't be concerned Alan, you worry too much."

"Yeah, right. Meet you down there at seven."

'See you then", said Sean, turning back to work on the roof repair. He was smiling now. Nearly finished with the repairs and was looking forward to getting back inside, drying off and having himself a celebratory beer or two.

CHAPTER 4

BEFORE

Monday 11 September 2017
Virginia Water England

Virginia Water is an exceedingly pretty village in leafy Surrey, home to the Wentworth Estate and the Wentworth Club. It is the most expensive place to live in the UK outside London. It took its name from the nearby Virginia Water Lake, which, it's claimed, is itself named after Elizabeth I, the Virgin Queen, though some doubt this story. Brandon and Fiona lived in a splendid six-bedroom property on Christchurch Road Virginia Water, a property far too big for their needs now. Despite many years of trying, they seemed destined to remain childless.

Brandon woke at 05:30 a.m. He went downstairs quietly, let the dog out into the garden, made himself some coffee then sat down at the kitchen table and fired up his laptop. He googled Irma Naples. Lots of information displayed on the page. He scanned the various reports, then breathed a huge sigh of relief when he read the byline underneath the CNN report. *No surge as predicted.* Clicking on the link he began to read the whole article, slurping his hot coffee as he did so. Cutting through the text he speed read then stopped and read more slowly.

'Much to the relief of the residents and the authorities of Naples, the predicted fifteen-foot tidal sea surge failed to materialize. In fact, the sea rose between only two to three feet, sparing most of the city of Naples from further destruction. But the increased sea level and torrential downpour is still causing massive damage to low lying trailer parks and other susceptible residential areas'. The article went on to describe other damage caused by the hurricane, but Brandon had read enough.

"Yippee," he shouted just as Fiona, his wife, walked into the kitchen.

"I thought I heard you get up. And what's all this "*yippee*" business? You certainly seem a lot happier than you did last night.

"I certainly am Fi. The storm surge didn't happen, well not enough to flood our condo, so it looks like we had a narrow escape."

"Good. So, when are you planning to go out there?"

"No rush now. I'll try to contact Mike Lee."

"Mike Lee? Have I met him, I don't recall?"

"Yes, you've met him, he's the manager. Now the worst is over I guess people will be going back there as soon as they can. I'll flirt off an email to tell him I'll be coming out there as soon as I can. So, how about some breakfast Fi? Suddenly I'm so hungry, I could eat a horse."

"Full English coming up," said his wife, happy now that Brandon was back in a good mood.

Two hours later Brandon was sitting at the kitchen table, head in his hands. He looked at his laptop and read the email again.

Hi Brandon.
Thanks for your email. And I'm sorry I haven't got any better news. This is an email I'm about send to all Roman Plaza residents.

Hi All
Roman Plaza and Irma
The good news was that the expected tidal surge didn't happen, the bad news is that Roman Plaza flooded anyway. The volume of water/rain overwhelmed the inadequate road drainage system and rainwater flooded into Roman Plaza When the water level fell, we got to work trying to salvage the situation. Apart from the few volunteers on hand, we had two men from the restoration company ripping out carpet and removing other stuff. We were expecting fans, water vacs and generators tomorrow, but then the power went out, apparently due to the flooding and no prospect of it coming back on soon. So, no air con, no water vacs, nothing. The situation is grim, and mold has already started to show.
The only thing we could do then was get some help in ripping

out all the interiors of the first-floor condos. All the drywall and sheetrock was removed in every apartment to prevent the mold spreading to the condos on the 2nd and 3rd floors. Basically, we had to take the ground floor condos back to the bare steel framework.
I apologize to the two absent ground floor owners, Brandon and Fiona Mellor and Otto and Hildegard Kellerman for not being able to give them prior warning. We had no choice and had to move fast. What valuable items we could see that were unaffected, plus computers and laptops etc., we moved to an empty 2nd floor condo for safe storage. What insurance relief we have will be compromised if we hadn't taken immediate action to limit the damage, and the most urgent matter now is to stop the spread of mold to the condos on the 2nd and 3rd floors.

I'll keep you updated.
PS, we're all remembering today, the victims of 9/11

Mike Lee
Manager

Fiona wandered back into the kitchen in her track suit.

"Phew it's muggy out there. Good run though, eight kilometers."

"What happened to miles?" Brandon replied in a curt tone.

"Oh dear, something bad happened darling?"

"You could say that."

"Do you want to tell me about it?"

"No, not now, go have your shower. I'll fill you in later." Fiona left him and went upstairs.

Brandon sat there deep in thought. He'd had one last ditch move to make, but the email from Mike Lee had all but wrecked that plan. Now, it looked like his 'get out of jail card' was gone. The only alternative he could think of was to sell the house, get his hands on some cash. *Even that might not be enough. I can't really sell the condo in Naples. If things get really bad, I'm going to need a bolt hole. Fiona loves this house and is never going to agree to sell. And what would I tell her, what reason could I give for having to sell? She'd never agree, never forgive my stupidity. She'll probably divorce me.*

"What the fuck am I going to do now?" he said out loud, then went over to the drinks cabinet, poured himself a large scotch and took a big swig of the amber liquid. He sat down, then hit his forehead with his hand.

"Of course! how dumb am I?" *I can remortgage the house. Must be, three, four million in equity at least. I cash some in. I don't have to tell Fiona, I can forge her signature well enough. Done it plenty of times before. I can get some capital back, invest in something solid but with a good return, pay some of the debt and keep those vicious bastards from doing anything stupid. Easy....* He had another drink of scotch, more slowly this time, smiled to himself and started working out how to execute his plan.

***

Far away, in Munich, Germany, some 750 miles to the southeast of Virginia Water, Otto and Hildegard Kellerman were reading Mike Lee's email with some trepidation and distress.

CHAPTER 5

TWO YEARS LATER

November 2019
St Peter the Apostle Catholic Church
Rattlesnake Hammock Rd, Naples

"Sean Kennedy was an honest man, a family man a hard-working artisan. He passed far too soon and will be sorely missed by his loving wife Sarah, his son Michael his daughter Elizabeth and all his many friends in the community...."

Father Aloysius Patrick McNulty droned on for another twenty minutes before finally ending his elaborate eulogy of a man he'd hardly known.

Michael leaned over and whispered to his sister.

"Artisan? What the fuck's an artisan? Dad was a drywaller wasn't he?"

She turned and cupping her hand over his ear to deaden her reply. She whispered back,

"It's a fancy word for Tradesman you ignorant fuckwit. Now shut up and stop asking stupid questions."

***

"That was a lovely service, a good sendoff Sarah," said the widow's friend Joyce. "Father McNulty's quite the eloquent one, isn't he?" Joyce continued as she shoveled another piece of pie into her mouth at the post funeral wake. "A bit inconsiderate of your Sean to die just before Christmas though."

"What!?" exclaimed the widow Kennedy.

"Sorry, thinking out loud. Must stop doing that." Sarah was about to respond in outrage but thought better of it. She had few enough friends as it was, without losing another, especially now. "Very easy on the eye too." Sarah looked at her friend nonplussed, then realized she'd switched back to Father McNulty.

"Shame he's taken a vow of celibacy," Joyce continued.

Sarah raised her eyebrows at Joyce's last remark.

"What?" asked Joyce. "have you heard things?"

"No, no, I haven't," replied Sarah, a little too firmly. Joyce was about to challenge her friend's response, but seeing the look on Sarah's face, decided against it. She changed the subject.

"Your Sean, I mean I know he liked a drink and I know you two didn't always see eye to eye," she said, "but he always brought home the bacon, didn't he? I mean, you two lived high off the hogg compared to the rest of us."

"We did that alright," replied the widow taking a gulp of her tea. "Makes you think though doesn't it, when someone dies, I mean? You know, what happens after?"

"After, how do you mean?"

"When you pass over. Do you pay for all the sins you committed in your life?" said Sarah.

"Don't think anyone ever came back to say, 'cept Jesus of course," said Joyce, "and he didn't commit any sins in the first place. Anyway, what makes you wonder about that? What have you got to feel guilty about?"

The widow didn't reply.

"More tea?" she said.

CHAPTER 6

PRESENT

February 2020 Naples Florida
Frankie Randazzo and Daisy

Frankie lived with his little dog Charlie in a first-floor apartment in the Acadiana condo complex in Naples, Florida. The previous year, Frankie's wife had once again decided that marriage to Frankie wasn't for her, and much to his regret, this eventually led to the commencement of bitter divorce proceedings.

They'd seemed happy enough since they'd been married, Frankie had thought, but then Penny suddenly declared out of the blue, that she was moving out and going to live with a female work colleague she'd fallen for. That floored Frankie. Eventually Penny decided she'd made a mistake and begged Frankie to give their marriage another go and let her come back. After some hesitation and much soul searching, Frankie agreed. Then a couple of years later, Penny once again showed signs of restlessness and one day declared she had to move out to go and 'find herself.' That had been the final straw for Frankie.

Frankie's second floor condo apartment looked down over the rear gardens and swimming pool of the Acadiana condo complex. It also had stunning views over Venetian Bay. He stood in his lanai, which had floor to ceiling window sliders. Opening one of the sliding windows, he breathed in the fresh morning air. Charlie sidled up to rub against his leg. Frankie bent down to pat Charlie's head, and the little dog's tail wagged in appreciation.

Frankie was back into his daily routine, a morning jog come walk with Charlie, shower and breakfast, then a catch up on emails from Derek Barns, *Barnsie*, his business partner in A & B Security in the UK. Subsequent work resulting from Derek's emails, usually took him up to lunchtime and after that he was free to do more or less as he pleased. His cell buzzed. He looked at the screen and thought he recognized the number.

"Hello."

"Is this Frankie Armstrong?" He definitely recognized the voice.

"It is," said Frankie. "Detective Randazzo I presume. How are you Sam?" Frankie walked over to the lanai and looked out over Venetian Bay. There were a couple of boats crossing the top of the bay, making their way towards Doctor's Pass and out into the Gulf of Mexico. *Great day to go fishing,* thought Frankie as he sat down. His little dog Charlie came to sit at his feet.

"I'm doing fine, thanks Frankie," the detective replied. "Leg's still a bit wonky. The doc says it'll probably never fully recover, but it's better than it was. I can live with it. Could have been much worse. You? How's that brain of yours functioning these days?

"Similar story. Getting better. The odd headache, plus my vision's still a bit off from time to time but definitely getting better."

"You were lucky Frankie. Bullet in the head. I still can't believe you got away with that."

"My business partner in the UK says it's because I only have a very small brain." Sam Randazzo laughed heartily at that.

Pleasantries over, Frankie was now wondering why Sam Randazzo was calling. He knew the detective wasn't the type to waste time just catching up, even if Frankie had saved his life. Before he could ask, Randazzo spoke again.

"So, to state the obvious, you're still here? In Naples I mean. You're still living in Acadiana in The Moorings, didn't go back to the UK yet?"

"No, I planned to, but then I couldn't work up the enthusiasm for an English winter, so here I am. Truth is, I'd like to live here permanently, but three months at a time is the maximum for a Brit on a visa waiver, so I guess I just have to make the most of it. I might try for a green card though."

"Well good luck with that. You're no doubt

wondering why I called?"

"Not just to ask after my health, correct?"

"You cynical bastard Frankie." Frankie waited. Randazzo laughed. "Okay, so I do have an ulterior motive which I'll tell you about in a minute, but I do wonder from time to time how you are. You still with your new love, Daisy, was it?"

"Yes, still together, well not exactly together as in living together, but..."

"Yeah, I get it. You ever get divorced?"

"Not so far. We're in the process, but the other party isn't being very cooperative at the moment. That was one of the things I really needed to go back home for. To sort that issue out. But maybe I can do most of it from out here?"

"Hmm, that's tough." There was a pause. Frankie spoke.

"Come on Sam, you said something about an ulterior motive. What's up, what is it you want? Hit me, as you American's say" Randazzo laughed.

"Okay. You only began renting your place in Acadiana from when, winter last year, 2019?"

"Yes why?"

"I need some information on the Moorings going back to September 2017 and maybe a short while before that."

"Information on what?"

"Sorry, on events near there in 2017."

"Events?"

"Yeah, more specifically, events relating to Hurricane Irma and how the aftermath played out at the Roman Plaza Condo complex. In particular, the flood that followed the actual hurricane."

"That big ornate place by the bridge?"

"The only one called Roman Plaza I think, though there might be another on Marco, but yes, the one by the bridge in the Moorings."

"Well, like you say, I wasn't here then but I do know about the hurricane of course and I know about the flood. I don't think it affected Acadiana that much, but I know it did do some damage to other properties nearby. But I don't see how I can help. And why Roman Plaza specifically anyway?"

"I have my reasons, but I'll explain later, okay?"

"Yeah, sure. But why not approach the president of the Roman Plaza Condominium, why not ask him, or her?"

"No, I really need, how can I put it, a more neutral source of information."

"You just want me to poke around there, see what I can find out?"

"Yeah, that would be good. But maybe be a bit discreet. You know what I mean?"

"Help if I knew what I'm looking for?"

"Might be nothing, but I've come across some information that makes me think some jewels could have been stolen from there. In the aftermath of the hurricane, I mean. Thing is, although they seem extremely valuable, I can't find any report of a theft of jewels anywhere around that time."

"You have these jewels then?"

"No, I have a picture that's all. Just poke around, see what you come up with and let's go from there. Could be just a wild goose chase. Just something that caught my interest is all. I know you're good at finding out stuff. So indulge me. Just do me a favor, and depending on what you come up with, we can then have a little chat and I'll elaborate, okay?"

"Okay, am I looking for anything about anyone in particular?"

"I don't know any names or details but that's the sort of thing I need to know. See what you can find out. No rush. Talk to you soon Frankie, keep well." Randazzo cut the line.

"Hmm," said Frankie as he sat reflecting on the conversation. Twice a week Frankie went to a boxing gym, The Big Hit, run by an ex-military guy called Gabriel Garcia, who everyone called Angel. Frankie did some weight training and an hour on the punchbag. He also did the occasional sparring round with Angel but had to be careful not to get any punches to the head because of his recent head trauma.

Angel wasn't tall, about 5'7' but was all muscle. Despite his slightly battered features, Angel seemed to be a magnet for the ladies. He oozed charm. He was also a bit of a joker and when asked how he got his nickname, he explained that his mom christened him Gabriel in the hope he would turn out to be somewhat saintlier than his dad, who at the time of Angel's birth, he claimed, was in the penitentiary for killing a man in a bar fight. No one knew if it was true, or a leg pull.

Angel and Frankie got on from the start, especially once they'd discovered that not only were they both ex-military but had both served in Iraq at the same time. Frankie in the British Army, Special Forces and Angel in the United States Marine Corps.

Today Frankie had some extra paperwork to do relating to his ongoing divorce from his wife Penny. Assets to divide. House to sell etc. His wife Penny now lived in their house back in the UK, whilst he was living in a long-term rental condo at The Acadiana in Naples. Dealing with the divorce and helping run his business based in the UK posed some complications. But he much preferred living out in Southern Florida, so wasn't trying too hard to get back to the UK.

Frankie's recovery from his head trauma the previous year was almost complete, with just the odd occasion when his vision became a little blurry, but these instances were in decline. He was looking forward to his date with Daisy tonight. Frankie could just sit and look at her forever. She was a cliché, natural blond hair, slim, shapely, light all over tan, clear brown - green eyes and as smart as a whip. She was so stunningly beautiful. Frankie wondered why she'd fallen for him, but decided not to ask too many questions, just accept his good luck.

Daisy was a reporter and they'd met when she came to interview him about the alligator attack the previous year. One thing had led to another, and they became an item. She was also a divorcee, so they'd agreed to keep living apart, and to some extent, live their own lives until they both felt able to commit further. That suited Frankie for the time being.

He was taking Daisy to Pepe's Pizza tonight so they could sit outside in the balmy Florida evening. The weather was perfect, a high of 80 degrees today, and a nighttime temperature forecast to be in the mid-seventies. In the meantime, there was hopefully some fishing to be done.

CHAPTER 7

PRESENT

Wednesday evening 19 February
Frankie and Daisy Pepe's Pizzeria

"So, why does the Detective Randazzo want you to find out what happened way back then, when Irma hit?" Daisy asked, "You weren't even living there then, so...?"

"I told him that, but he still wants me to ask around. He wants me to focus on Roman Plaza, you know, those condos by the bridge."

"Why doesn't he just go find out himself?" Frankie shrugged his Shoulders.

"I asked him that and I don't know. But I'll do as he asks and see where it goes. It's not as if I'm overwhelmed with things to do right now, so it'll keep me busy, and it might be interesting. But Sam's obviously up to something."

"Hmm, very mysterious," Daisy said. "Keep me posted, but in the meantime," she wiggled her empty glass in front of him.

"Oops, sorry," said Frankie as he poured her another glass of Merlot.

"So, what else have you been up to since I saw you last Friday?" she asked.

"Well, I've applied to the Green Card Lottery," replied Frankie.

"The what?" said Daisy,

"The Green Card Lottery,"

"I had no idea there was such a thing, and me a journalist. Explain."

"Okay, well a few days ago I was talking to a guy in a bar in Venetian Village, you know the open air one, belongs to that fish restaurant, which looks really good so we have to try it sometime. Where was I? Oh yeah and I was asking him how I might be able to stay in Florida permanently without first getting a job. I was telling him it seems a bit tricky, you need a job to get a green card, but you need a green card to get a job. He asked me if I'd tried applying through the Green Card Lottery. I looked into it, and it turns out they randomly grant over 50,000 green cards every year to people who apply. So, I thought, what's to lose?"

"Wow, well here's hoping Frankie," she said clinking her glass against his. And here comes the pizza." They each took a large slice of pizza and between bites, carried on their conversation.

"You really love it here don't you Frankie, Naples I mean."

"What's not to like? It has everything, great weather, beautiful beaches, fishing, nice friendly people, great restaurants etc. etc. Can't think of many places like it."

"You're not on your own there Frankie, do you know how many millionaires there are in Naples?"

"No idea, but a lot I'd guess."

"Well, I recently had to write a feature on the subject and even I was surprised, and I've lived here most of my life. About 10% of the Naples population are millionaires, which is impressive. Believe it or not, there are about 12,300 millionaire households in Naples. That's a lot considering population is just over 300,000."

"Twelve thousand millionaires, in Naples!?"

"You betcha! and then there's the billionaires like Shahid Kahn, one of the richest guys in the US of A."

"Woah enough already Daisy. I feel like pauper as it is. And by the time my wife gets finished with me I'll likely qualify for welfare."

"Okay, but we also have our fair share of celebs as well, Judge Judy, Sean Hannity, Bob Seger. You know Naples was also one of Gary Cooper's favorite places?"

"I didn't. Shame, I can't do Gary Cooper. I can do a passable John Wayne though," Frankie said.

"Spare me," said Daisy laughing. "So apart from the mysterious request from Randazzo and the green card thing, anything else happening?"

"Nope, just the usual, business back in the UK is good, my divorce drags on and on. Other than that I've been taking it easy, hanging round the pool, chewing the fat, you know," Frankie stopped talking."

"What?"

"Well, there was something a bit odd. Didn't take much notice at the time, but..."

"Come on Frankie, what was odd?"

"Something and nothing really, just this young guy came down to the pool the other day. I was on my own doing a few laps. So, when I got out of the pool, he starts a conversation, nothing notable, just the usual, 'lovely day,' that sort of stuff 'lived here long,' you know, just small talk, anyway he put his towel on a sunbed and sunbathed for a while. I did the same and fell asleep."

"When I woke up a few of the other residents had come down and we said Hi to each other. I looked around for the young guy and he was gone, so I asked the others who he was. It was unusual for such a young guy to be at Acadiana, not used to seeing anyone under fifty. Normally much older. And, I've just realized, his accent, I'd swear it wasn't American. Something else..."

"So...?"

"So, no one else had seen any young guy, and I haven't seen him since."

"You said he didn't sound American, anything else unusual?"

"Well, I suppose he had a bit of a darkish complexion, but that might have been a really deep suntan."

"Maybe he was a guest of one of the residents, or one of their kids visiting?"

"Yeah, you're probably right; Frankie shook his head, "just something, I don't know...the way he looked at me?"

"You and your suspicious mind." Daisy said.

"Yeah, you're probably right." Frankie replied. They were sitting outside Pepe's Pizza restaurant in Naples Florida on the Gulf of Mexico. It was 7.00 p.m. on a Tuesday evening in mid-June. The air temperature was perfect, high seventies. Daisy took another slice of pizza from the serving dish and plonked it on Frankie's plate.

"More wine?" she asked and proceeded to pour without waiting for his answer. Frankie laughed.

"Supposing I didn't want any more wine?" he said.

"Then I'd know you weren't really Frankie Armstrong, but a robot sent to earth by alien beings, so they could study at close hand, the most beautiful creature they had ever seen." She topped up her own glass, put the bottle down and took a bite of her pizza. Frankie looked round in an exaggerated fashion. "Don't say it if you want to live buster," Daisy said chewing on her food and looking serious. Frankie laughed.

"What?" he said, "anyway, as it happens," he continued keeping a straight face, "I am indeed an alien and will want to conduct some experiments on you later. These will of course require you to divest yourself of earthly clothing so we can do some intimate response testing."

"We?" Daisy said and started to laugh so hard she nearly choked on her food. Frankie's face cracked and he started to laugh as well, attracting attention from the other diners.

"Behave yourself," said Daisy as they both got themselves under control.

"Men!" Daisy said, raising her eyes to heaven, "can't keep your minds off sex for five minutes."

"Gosh, has it been that long?" said Frankie looking at his watch, d'you know any way of curing the urge?" Daisy smiled.

"I might," she said, "but I only offer treatment on Tuesdays." Frankie started to count the days of the week on his hands.

"Looks like it's my lucky day then," he said trying to suppress a grin.

"Well so it is, said Daisy draining the last of her wine, "better get the bill. You seem in quite a desperate state. The sooner we begin treatment the better I think," she said, stifling a giggle.

CHAPTER 8

PRESENT

Thursday 20 February 2020
Pools of knowledge

Frankie had been doing a gentle backstroke in the pool, trying to think how he could casually bring up the subject of Hurricane Irma, but couldn't think of anything other than the direct approach. He walked up the steps and out of the pool and stood by his sun lounger toweling himself dry. He looked around. There were, as usual, a number of Acadiana residents in or around the pool, variously chatting or reading or just sunbathing.

"So, tell me the story of what happened, you know, after hurricane Irma hit? Someone said that the Roman Plaza place was hit badly." *Subtle as a sledge hammer.* He hadn't addressed anyone in particular, but Linda Monastery was the nearest, sitting on the steps of the pool.

"What made you bring that subject up Frankie?" asked Linda.

"Oh, just wondered. Heard someone the

other day talking about the damage Irma did to some nearby condo places."

"Well, that's where you're wrong Frankie, said Tony Yassaman, who was sitting under a large sun umbrella at one of poolside tables "the hurricane itself just caused some relatively minor damage No, the real damage was done by the rain and floods afterwards. The rain after the hurricane was heavy and nonstop, it flooded the roads. The drains couldn't cope with all that water in such a short time. We were lucky here, but some other places were hit bad. It was an accident waiting to happen."

"We'd all complained to the city before about the drains, but as usual no one took any notice. I think they were one of the worst hit. Next time you walk to the bridge, just notice how the road dips in the section just outside Roman Plaza."

"If you really want to know more, go speak to Mike Lee," said Meg, "he's the manager of Roman Plaza now. Used to be manager here before our president decided we needed to tighten our belts and he let him go. Nice guy Mike, Shame he went." Meg suddenly stopped talking, forgetting her thread. "What was I saying?" she said to Frankie. Frankie smiled.

"You were telling me about Mike Lee and the Roman Plaza condos."

"Oh yes, Mike, nice man. If you want to know about what happened there, you should go talk to Mike, he'd tell you. But you still haven't said why you want to know what happened."

"Just put it down to my eccentric British curiosity." Both Meg and Tony Yassaman looked at him, obviously not buying his explanation one bit. He decided to leave the pool to avoid any further questions and having to make up idiotic answers. He bid them all goodbye and left.

A few minutes later he was walking down Harbour Drive in the direction of the bridge which carried the road over a narrow stretch of Venetian Bay. He often stopped at the bridge when he was out walking Charlie, to take in the view or to watch the passage of boats as they made their way to or from Doctors Pass coming in or going out into the Gulf of Mexico. On the left-hand side of the road, just before the bridge was the Roman Plaza condo complex.

As the name suggested, Roman Plaza was built in mock Romanesque Italianate style with semi naked statues of Roman gods dotted around the perimeter. In the center of a mini roundabout at the entrance stood a magnificent large bronze rendition of a Roman soldier, wearing a helmet, armor, standing in a chariot with reins and whip in hand, charging at some imaginary foe. *Don't you just love a bit of over-the-top architecture?* He made his way round the back of the complex to seek out manager Mike Lee. *Wonder if he'll be dressed aa a Roman centurion?*

"Can I help you sir? A voice asked. Frankie turned to his left and encountered a man dressed in shorts, light blue shirt with an emblem Roman Plaza embroidered in red on it.

"I was looking for Mike Lee the manager."

"You found him. What can I help you with?"

"Hi Mike," said Frankie, "I'm Frankie Armstrong, I live, well I long term rent, in Acadiana just up the road a piece, on the other side."

"Yeah, I know where Acadiana is, used to be manager there before I moved here. Nice place, great crowd. You thinkin' of moving here instead?" he said eyebrows raised a little.

"No, no, nothing like that, just wondered if you could tell me about what happened when Irma struck. I mean what happened to the Roman Plaza complex after the hurricane?"

"I don't understand, why are you asking about that?" Frankie had prepared an excuse, weak but might just about believable.

"Daisy Metcalf, she's a reporter, a local journalist. She writes article for the Naples Daily News sometimes. You might have read some of her stuff."

"I think I recognize the name, so maybe I have."

"Well, she and I are an item. Have been for a while. Anyway, she's really swamped at the moment, so she asked me to do some research on Irma three years on. She's doing a piece on hurricanes in general. How they impact Florida and its residents, that sort of thing."

"Okay," he said somewhat skeptically, "so what is it you want to know?"

"How much damage Irma inflicted on Roman Plaza. I'm led to believe you were flooded out."

"And then some," said Mike. "Listen, I have to go on an errand, maybe you'd be better talking to some of the residents. There should be a few of them around the pool at the moment. Normally is about this time. I'll take you round, introduce you and then I'll have to go."

"You're very kind Mr. Lee."

"Mike please. Come on, follow me."

Mike took him round the corner of the building where there was a pool, similar to the one in Acadiana, except this one had a straw roofed circular Tikki bar to one side. Sure enough there were a few of the residents in the pool or around it variously reading and sunbathing or talking.

"Hey folks, this is..." he looked at Frankie.

"Frankie."

"Yeah, this is Frankie and he's looking for information on what happened to this place after Irma struck. I'll leave him to explain I gotta go. Bye folks."

"Bye Mike" came the response.

"Take a seat Frankie, said one of the men standing in the pool. Frankie grabbed a poolside chair and sat. The man who'd invited him to sit down introduced himself and the others around or in the pool.

"I'm Terry Heitmann, this here's," pointing to his left, "Mike Price and Jen Perry. Those two sunbathing there are Paul and Teresa Blankenship and that guy over there is Rudy Christman" They all either did a little wave or said Hi. "Now what is it you want to know Frankie?" Frankie explained to them what he was looking for. He knew once they started, they'd be hard to stop. One thing he'd learnt is that retired people who live in these places are always looking to break the boredom. The man called Rudy spoke first.

"Well, you're right about the floods causing the most damage. See the road outside here is a low point and the water just poured into the car park, inundated the first-floor condos, swamped the cars. In the end every one of the first-floor condos here had to be completely rebuilt inside and all the cars were all write offs."

"Wasn't just the water either though, was it Terry?" said Jen Perry, "the water caused the power supply to go down. Before that happened, they probably could've pumped out the water and dried the places out before the mold took hold. But the power went off and that was that. That mold grew faster than green grass goes through a goose."

"Sure did, yes siree," said Rudy Christian who'd now moved closer to join in. "We were lucky that Mike Lee took swift decisive action to get the places stripped out there and then. It upset a few folks who thought he shoulda waited for formal permission from the condo owners, the ones who were absent at the time I mean."

"Yeah," said Jen Perry, "We were here, so it wasn't a problem. All the first-floor residents that were here at the time didn't want any delay. We all had to move out for a while, so that was a big inconvenience. But the condo owners who weren't here then couldn't appreciate the urgency. The English guy Brandon, he was really pissed I heard. Otto was as well. Both of 'em gave Mike a really hard time, his wife told me."

"Understandable I guess," said Rudy Christman, "but if Mike hadn't moved fast, then the whole block would have been infected with mold. Can you imagine what would have happened then?"

"Hey Terry, I think Otto's due back here tomorrow or the next day, isn't he? Be nice to see him. Been a while."

"I didn't know that, so yeah be great to see him." Replied Terry. "Mind you, we won't see that much of him anyway. He'll be off on one of his little cruises. I mean I like a cruise, who doesn't, but I never met anyone who loves cruising as much as the Kellermans."

"And the annoying thing is," said Paul Blankenship as she sat on the steps at the shallow end of the pool, "They never put any weight on. Every cruise I been on, I put on at least ten pounds.

They come back looking as slim as always."

"Yeah, I noticed that too, really annoying," said Jen Perry, "I think it's the Mediterranean diet, they don't eat all the crap we American's do."

"How many ground floor units are there?" asked Frankie trying to get the conversation back on track.

"Ten altogether," replied Jen Perry.

"And all ten were badly affected by the flood waters?"

"Destroyed more like," said Terry, "when I say they had to be stripped out, I mean gutted."

"They were, completely ruined," said Jen, "once you get mold, you gotta strip out everything and I mean everything. The furniture, carpets, kitchen, even the walls. The condos had to be taken back to the bare bones, well in this case, the metal stud wall frames."

"So, the actual interior walls were taken out?"

"Yup, its sheetrock," she said "and mold just loves to grow on sheetrock. So, like Terry said, everything was stripped out. But on the good side, all the ground floor owners got their places completely remodeled, courtesy of the insurance company and the FEMA fund."

"FEMA?" asked Frankie.

'Yeah, the disaster relief fund. It's called FEMA but don't ask me why."

"I know," said Teresa Blankenship.

"Why am I not surprised," muttered Terry,

under his breath.

"It stands for Federal Emergency Management Agency," she said, smiling now, obviously pleased with herself. Terry started swimming lengths of the pool.

"Any other damage." Asked Frankie, "anything went missing at all?"

"Why do you ask if anything went missing?" "No reason, just you know, sometimes unscrupulous people take advantage of a crisis, steal things while folks are distracted, that sort of thing."

"Well, I wouldn't say we don't have any unscrupulous people in this neck of the woods, but stealing? Nah. Least not as far as I know. Anyone else know about any burglarizing at that time?" Paul Blankenship asked looking around at them all?" No one answered. Only thing was, anyone who had a car parked here got it written off," he said.

"Including us," chipped in Rudy Christman, "we'd only had the car a week, A brand new Lexus, written off just like that!"

Frankie couldn't think what else to ask, so decided to leave. He thanked them all for their help and they said he was welcome back any time. Frankie walked back to Acadiana, went to his condo and made notes of what he'd been told, or as much as he could remember. He couldn't imagine any of the information he'd gleaned would be particularly useful to Randazzo, *but what do I know?* thought Frankie.

CHAPTER 9

PRESENT

Friday 21February 2020

Randazzo calls

Frankie rose with the sun. He looked out his bedroom windows at the calm clear morning, the water shimmering like glass, sunlight gilding the tops of the bayside properties. A fish rose and created a ring of ripples. An osprey circled the water in search of prey. He stayed very still for a few moments before turning round and making for the door to go for his regular morning jog around Venetian Bay with Charlie. The weather, as usual, was sunny and warm. Frankie jogged past pedestrians on the sidewalk, variously speed walking or just taking an early morning stroll with their dogs. He invariably got a 'good morning', a wave and a smile... *Naples..*

Back at his condo, he fed Charlie, showered, breakfasted, then went on to his PC to read his emails, most of which he deleted. There were some social emails from the few friends who still kept in touch. Once he'd replied to those, he studied the emails from his business partner in the UK.

Frankie read the sales reports, the financials and Derek's proposals for discussion on some business developments he'd been thinking about. Frankie emailed back with some comments and suggestions, ending with a promise to call or Skype Derek later in the day. Frankie stood up went to the kitchen and re-filled his coffee mug, then went and stood in the lanai. He never tired of looking out at the view over Venetian Bay.

He could see a few of his neighbors already out around the pool, either sunbathing, or reading, or bobbing around in the water chatting. The conversational subjects around the pool ranged widely but typically focused on recent restaurant visits or meals cooked. Food played a large part in the lives of retired folks in Florida. Turning away from the view, he grabbed his cell off the coffee table and tapped in a number. The detective answered on the third ring.

"Frankie Armstrong, how are you?"

"Fine Sam., I did as you suggested, went to Roman Plaza yesterday and spun them a yarn about doing some research for Daisy about an article she was writing on hurricanes. I met the manager Mike Lee and asked some folks some questions about what happened when Irma struck, and about the flooding afterwards, but I doubt any of the information I got will be any use to you.

"Yeah, maybe, maybe not. But first tell me what you found out. We'll take it from there, okay?"

Frankie sighed, picked up the notes he'd made and told the detective what he'd found out. Randazzo stopped him and asked the odd question for clarification, but for most part he just listened. Frankie finished his report.

"That's it. Like I said not much, but there it is. Is this something that helps in any way. Maybe you'd be better going to talk to them yourself, or send another detective?"

"Maybe, but the truth is, I'm kinda doing this off the books as you might say."

"Oh?" said Frankie. "How so?"

"I'd rather come around and tell you in person. You busy at the moment?"

"No, not particularly."

"I'll see you in half an hour, get the coffee on."

CHAPTER 10

PRESENT

Friday 21 February 2020
Detective Randazzo

The detective arrived forty minutes later. Frankie noticed the limp was still evident.

"Take a seat at the dining table, easier to talk there," said Frankie noticing a faint whiff of booze as the detective brushed past him to sit down.

"The leg improved any?"

"Yeah, some, but I won't be chasing any criminals like I used to, least not on foot. You know, I could outrun most guys half my age till that crazy bastard put a bullet in my leg."

"Yeah, well look on the bright side Sam, that lunatic could've easily killed you, the state he was in."

"Well, you're right and I guess that's down to

you buddy. So, is that coffee on?"

Frankie went to pour the coffee, came back and they sat round the dining table. Charlie walked over and lay at Frankie's feet.

"Such a cute little pooch," Randazzo said, "he really loves you Frankie. I keep meaning to talk to my wife about getting one."

"If you're serious, then do it. I never had a dog before Charlie and now...Someone once said, 'If you want a true friend in life, get a dog".

"Amen to that," said the detective and took a sip of his coffee. "You make good coffee Frankie." Frankie nodded his appreciation. "Okay, well, a couple of weeks ago this lady, a Mrs. Kennedy, she came to the police department to report something, and I happened to be in the front office at the time, otherwise it wouldn't have gone anywhere, still might not. The desk Sergeant is always a bit cynical of people who wander in to 'report something'." Randazzo said making air quotes. "Can't blame the guy."

"He gets all kinds of weirdos coming in to report stuff. 'Men from Mars have just landed and kidnapped their buddy', you know the kind of thing. So, he listens to what she said and made some notes. I'd been listening in. Just my nosy nature I guess, but she started by saying she wanted to confess something. I couldn't see his face, but my guess is he rolled his eyes. I certainly heard him sigh in the fashion of *not another one.* Okay he says, if you can you give me some basic details. Then he wrote down her name address, telephone etc., all the usual stuff, you know."

"When he'd done that, he asked her what she wanted to confess to. She hesitated as if she'd changed her mind, but then she said it was about her husband. Said he'd died last November. Said she was sure he'd stolen some valuable stuff, diamonds, jewelry and stuff. The sergeant asked her when this was. She said it was a few years ago, late 2017. Said they'd been living life better than they should have since then. The husband, he just didn't earn that sort of money. They'd had expensive vacations, new furniture and things. Said she was worried he was gambling, or maybe borrowing money. Said she asked him, and he just laughed and said she shouldn't worry."

"Anyway, she said she looked in all the places he hid things. Thought she didn't know where he hid stuff. She said he'd always been a bit light fingered, thought he stole stuff whenever he could, but only small stuff, and sold it to friends. Said he was clever and never got caught as far as she knew. But this time she found some jewelry. Said it looked expensive, really expensive. The sergeant asked her if she'd brought it with her. She seemed flustered, then said she hadn't because when she went to look for it, it was all gone."

"He asked her if she had any idea where he'd stolen it from and if she thought anyone else was involved in the theft. She said she had no idea where it came from. That her husband was a builder, a handyman. Mainly did drywall stuff. And she said she didn't know if anyone else was involved, but she didn't think there was. The sergeant then asked her how her husband died, was there anything suspicious, anything to link his death with this jewelry did she think."

"At last, an intelligent question I thought. So, this Mrs. Kennedy replied no. Said the autopsy report said natural death, his heart. It said he had a lot of alcohol in his system which they thought could have been a contributory factor, or something like that. So, the sergeant says, if he passed last November, why wait so long to come and report all this. She explains she'd been busy getting things organized. That Sean, her husband, had left their affairs in a bit of a mess. And then there's the grief, she said knocked her and the kids sideway. Said she was only just coming to terms with it all. Then she started crying and the sergeant handed her a tissue."

"I'm really sorry for your loss ma'am, says the sergeant, then carries on 'Look, Mrs. Kennedy, he says, without evidence, or any idea where this jewelry came from or who took it, it's just a story. And the only person we could have asked about it, has passed away. Have you any idea at all who might have taken it from where your husband had hidden it?"

"No, nobody knew his hiding places except me, that I'm sure of. But I thought I had to come and tell you,' She said, it's been on my mind a lot, so I decided get it off my conscience. My husband died in a state of sin. I don't want to meet my maker in the same way. So here I am. I knew when we started living the good life that something wasn't right. I should have done something about it then, but I didn't. I succumbed to temptation, and I want to make it right with God."

"Ma'am are you a Catholic? asked the sergeant. A fair guess I thought considering her name. As soon as he asked her that, I knew where I'd seen her before. She goes to the same church as I do. Anyway, she nodded, and he said 'Then my advice is to go to your priest, confess then do your penance or whatever it is, then you just forget about it. But I'll make a report just in case you remember anything else about the jewelry, or better still, find it. If you do, you come back and tell us, okay?"

"Okay she said, thanks for listening, then she sobbed a little more and went out the door. The sergeant left to go to the restroom, so I looked at the report on the counter and made a note of her contact details."

"So, you reckon this Sean Kennedy, this is the guy who stole the jewels? And you're wondering if he worked on the condos in Roman plaza after the flood damage. And you're wondering if he stole some valuable jewels from a condo in Roman Plaza. But no one has reported the theft of valuable jewelry from Roman Plaza, or anywhere else presumably? So, why are you pursuing this 'off the books?'" said Frankie making the air quotes again. "Why are you pursuing this at all? You must have enough official reported crime to keep you busy. So why the interest in this?" The detective took a long swig of his coffee.

"I don't know, a feeling, a hunch, I guess. I admit I can get a little obsessive about stuff. You know, when something just gets under your skin? Listen, I'm probably wasting my time, and yours too. But let me tell you the rest of it, then it might make a bit more sense."

"Okay, but give me your cup, I think we need more coffee." Frankie got two more cups of coffee, sat down and took a sip. Randazzo sipped at his, breathed out.

"Say, you got anything to liven this up with? said Randazzo holding his cup out.

"Liven it up?" Randazzo raised his eyebrows cocked his head and looked at Frankie. "Oh, right, yes, whisky okay?" the detective nodded.

"That'll do it," said Randazzo. Frankie got the whisky and poured a slug into the detective's coffee cup. He tasted it, "ahh, that's better," he said, "You not joining me?"

"Bit early for me Sam. You were saying."

"Yeah, where was I? Yeah right, so I'd thought about it overnight and decided to take it further." Frankie raised his eyebrows. "Yeah, I know, but whatever. So, rather than go see the woman directly, I went to talk to the priest, Father McNulty. He's a nice guy, bit too good looking for a priest though. The women nearly swoon when he dishes out the communion hosts, though that's on hold at the minute, the virus. So, I asked him if Mrs. Kennedy, Sarah Kennedy's her full name. I asked him what he thought of her. Would he trust anything she said? He said she was a straight shooter, a bit blunt at times, but sharp as a tack."

"I then asked him if he thought she was capable of making things up, was she badly affected emotionally by the death of her husband? He said if anything, she was the steady one in the relationship. Honest and direct in his experience. Said he didn't want to speak ill of the dead, but he thought Sean was a bit on the shady side. Nothing he knew of in particular, just a feeling he got about the man. I thanked him and asked him to keep our conversation private."

"Having been told by McNulty that Sarah Kennedy was unlikely to be some sort of fantasist I decided to go see her." Randazzo stopped and took a gulp of coffee, then continued. "They live in a one-story single-family home on the north side of the 41. Tidy garden and so on. She answered the door and I introduced myself. The priest was right, she was sharp all right."

"You're the guy from the police station, she said, I could tell you were listening in. That sergeant took all the details so why you are here, what do you want? I'm curious,' says I. "You going to invite me in?" She hesitated then opened the door and let me in. She showed me into the kitchen, then made coffee for us both. Curiosity killed the cat, she said, so what do you want to know Mr. Detective? All defensive and a little bit hostile. I asked her some questions, then asked to see where her husband had hidden the alleged stolen jewelry. She showed me his hiding place. It was in their bedroom. To get to it, you had to remove the bottom drawer of a set of drawers, then lift a floorboard underneath that. It was a neat place, very difficult to find unless you knew it was there. There was nothing in it of course. We went back to the kitchen, and I asked her if she could describe the jewelry. I made notes."

"I only saw it briefly, but there were two pieces. One was like a big star shape with lots of diamonds. Even in the darkness of the hidey hole, the stones sparkled like nothing I've ever seen before. I asked her what size this first piece was. She used her hands and I reckoned she was describing something about four to five inches overall. The second piece, she said, was a bit smaller, with a crown thing at the top and kind of oval shape underneath, like a big pendent."

"I can tell when someone's lying, and she wasn't, least not about that anyway. But there was something a bit off. But I knew this was something real, something potentially very valuable maybe, but without getting my hands on it...? Then I had a brainwave. Sorry Frankie, I need the rest room."

Frankie told him where it was.

CHAPTER 11

PRESENT

Friday 21 February 2020
Detective Randazzo

Sam Randazzo returned to his seat opposite Frankie at the dining table.

"Okay, where was I?"

"Brainwave," said Frankie.

"Yeah right. So, I said I assumed her husband had a cell phone. She said he did, but it's passworded, she said, and none of us knew what the password was, so Michael, our son, he said he'd like to have it. It was one of those fancy iPhones. So, he's taken it to the mall, not more than half an hour ago. He said he's going to get it re-set or get a new sim card so he can use it. Just then we hear someone come in the front door. 'That'll be him now."

"So, this young guy comes into the room and his mother introduces me. So, I'm just hoping he hasn't had the phone wiped. 'The detective here wants to ask you about pop's iPhone,' she says. And he says, it's here but pop's stuff isn't on it any more. Shit! I think. Did you get it wiped or get a new sim? I asked. New sim. The guy said it was best in the circumstances. Anyway, long story short. Thankfully, he'd brought the old sim back home with him, intending to ask his mother before throwing in the trash or destroying it."

"And where does this get you exactly Sam?"

"Man, I love it when it all comes together," said Randazzo with an unusual display of enthusiasm. "I took it back to HQ and asked one of the techies to download any pictures that were on the phone."

"Sean had photographed the jewelry?!"

"You got it Frankie. One picture only, showing both pieces. Not a great photographer our Sean. Worse than me, but you can see enough. Man, I could see what she meant. Even with the crappy picture, you could see they were stunning pieces of jewelry. All the gemstones seemed intact on both pieces, but I guess you'd have to see them up close to make sure." The detective took out his cell phone and scrolled through, then held the screen up for Frankie to see.

"Wow, I see what you mean. What does your chief say?"

"Haven't told anyone yet. See, first I did some research on thefts of jewelry. Now I knew what I was looking for, I guessed it wouldn't be too difficult to find out where the stuff came from, but I came up with nothing, nada, zilch! How weird is that? I mean, stuff like this would be on the police computer for sure, wherever it had been lifted from. But nothing."

"So, what does that tell you?" asked Frankie, stolen somewhere abroad maybe?"

"Possible, but unlikely seeing how a relatively local low life had got his hands on it. Had to be from somewhere not a million miles away from here. No, there's only two reasons a theft of something like this wouldn't show up. Either the person who it was stolen from doesn't know yet - unlikely, or..." The detective said nothing waiting for Frankie to think it through. Frankie looked at Sam who merely raised his eyebrows and smiled expectantly. A few seconds passed.

"It was stolen goods already?! They couldn't report it!"

"You got it." replied Sam.

CHAPTER 12

PRESENT

Friday 21February 2020
Randazzo and Frankie

"I still don't get why you're so sure the Roman Plaza Condo complex comes into this scenario Sam."

"It might not. But I also got Sean's telephone contact numbers, so maybe we can check on what properties he'd been working on and where, in the period immediately prior to when the Kennedys started to live 'better than they should', as Mrs. Kennedy put it. Make sure my hunch holds up. See I went back to show Sarah Kennedy the picture, just to make sure. She confirmed that was the piece of jewelry she'd seen hidden in Sean's hiding place."

"I guess she appreciated the phone picture confirming her story."

"You'd think so, but she didn't seem that thrilled somehow. She thanked me for going to the trouble to come back to her though. She also told me to tell that *Son of a bitch desk sergeant* that he was an asshole for the way he talked to her *condescending bastard* I think was the precise term she used. I said I'd think about that, and she laughed. I took the opportunity to ask her if she knew where Sean had been working at the time, she thought he may have taken the jewels. But she said he didn't always tell her where he was working, so we need to check further."

"His phone records could be handy in finding out where he did jobs during that time. He always worked as a sub-contractor, she said, so in effect was always working for some other tradesman or company. All we need to do is call everyone he contracted with to try to establish which properties or houses has working on then." Sam added.

"But she said she did recall he worked on a condo complex on Harbour Drive just after the hurricane. She couldn't remember which one at first, but then she said she thought it was called Rome something. I asked if she meant Roman Plaza. I know the place 'cos the statues make me laugh every time I drive past it, especially the guy in the chariot. She said that was it. She remembers because it was such an emergency due to the damage the hurricane and the flooding had caused. Sean had said it was urgent and it was also good pay. Says he asked her to help out by calling one of his existing commitments to say he'd be delayed getting to them."

"Well, that sounds promising then. But, you said 'we' need to check further?" said Frankie, emphasizing the 'we'.

"Yeah, well. Thing is I'd still like to keep this off the books for the time being. I need more if I'm going to make this official. All I have now, is a story and a picture, nothing solid. So, I thought you might be interested in helping out?"

"And why would I do that Sam?

"Okay, well as a favor to me, and you're good at this sort of stuff. In another life you'd have made a great detective. Look at how you found that guy in the UK, despite him adopting a new identity."

"Yes, but I had motivation for that Sam. As you know only too well, he killed someone I loved."

"Yeah, I know, and this is obviously different. But don't tell me you're not intrigued? And it wouldn't take up much of your time. I just need to establish if this has legs. Once I do, I can go official with it. You in?"

Frankie looked at the detective and shook his head.

"I must be crazy. Okay Sam I'm in. Where do I

start?"

"Well, I reckon finding out what these jewels are would be good. They're quite distinctive, so maybe a top-notch antique jewelry person might know?"

"Agreed, just let me grab a pen and my notepad and I'll make some notes as we go along."

"Okay," said Frankie returning to his seat. "Find antique jewelry expert", Frankie said as he wrote. "Course they might not be that old?"

"I think they're old. And that seems like a crown shape on the smaller piece. Looks kinda regal to me," said Randazzo.

Frankie looked again at the picture on the detective's phone.

"You're right Sam, it does. Can you send the picture to my email?"

"Sure thing," said Randazzo and took the phone back from Frankie and tapped away for a few seconds, then handed it back. "On its way."

Frankie took the phone back and studied the picture again.

"Okay, I'll look at that on my PC when you've gone, see if I can improve the picture any. Next?"

"The when. When did Sean lift the jewelry? We know it was around the time of hurricane

Irma or just after maybe. So, we need to find out what and where Sean was working at that time in a bit more detail."

"If you can get the phone numbers off his phone, that would help me find out."

"Yep, I'll get that arranged. I'll get my pet techie to download the numbers, load 'em up on a spreadsheet then email it over to you."

"Okay," said Frankie, anything else?"

"No, I think we got enough to be going on with. Let's see how you go on and we'll meet up again when you have something to report."

"Okay Sam. On another matter, are you okay? I mean..., well I don't want to stick my nose in, but...the booze?"

"Yeah, I know. Martha keeps on at me about it too. It's the leg and I don't know. The pain, the pain reminds me of when that fucking lunatic shot me. A little drink now and then and the odd painkiller helps a bit. I don't overdo it, okay, so no need to worry about me."

"Maybe you're suffering a bit of delayed PTS?" The detective looked puzzled, Frankie carried on talking. "It's only that I had it after I'd left the army. I didn't realize till one day my wife Penny suggested that was what was wrong with me. She said I'd been short tempered and snappy all the time, not like me at all. I said no, but eventually I talked to someone, and they helped me work my way through it." The detective looked at Frankie, stroked his chin and spoke.

"I don't think so Frankie, but I'll think on what you said, okay?"

"I hope you don't think I've spoken out of turn Sam."

"No, I understand Frankie. No offence taken." They both stood and the detective made for the door, then turned around. "I really appreciate your help with this investigation, Frankie."

"No trouble Sam. Got to admit, I am intrigued."

Same waved his hand in the air as he turned, opened the door and left. Frankie sat back down for a minute and reflected on all they'd discussed, *hope Sam's okay.* He shrugged, stood up and went and made himself another coffee. Back at his PC, he checked his email and copied the picture of the jewelry from Randazzo's email message and placed on his desktop. He opened it up in his picture viewer and zoomed in. The picture wasn't the best and blurred as he enlarged it. He needed someone to help seriously improve the quality of the picture. He hadn't got the expertise himself, but he knew a man who had.

CHAPTER 13

PRESENT

Friday 21 February 2020
Randazzo

Sam Randazzo left Frankie's condo and drove down to Old Naples, parked his car at the back of Fifth Avenue and strolled down fifth to Clive's Bar and Grill. He took a high seat at the bar and watched the busy waiters and waitresses serving the lunchtime crowd, chatting away. Some lone office workers, one couple deep in conversation, another couple a little more distant studying their menus *had they argued, or were they just bored with each other*?

There were family groups with small children misbehaving. Groups of older tourists, relaxed and enjoying their vacations, sitting at the tables on the sunny sidewalk laughing and joking and drinking. Life looked pretty good in Naples. Clive came down the bar to where the detective sat. A bar towel draped over his shoulder.

"How's it going Sam? The usual, bourbon?"

"I guess so Clive, make it a big one, lots of ice." His drink came. He reached in his pocket and pulled out a plastic container, shook two pills from it, put them in his mouth, then washed the pills down with a swig of the amber liquid. Closing his eyes, he waited.

"Ahh, that's better" he said leaning back. and rubbing his leg. Clive came back along the bar drying some glasses and placing them on a shelf.

"That leg still giving you gyp?" Clive asked him.

"Yeah, it's a bitch. Can't sleep much. These help," said Randazzo rattling the pill tube before placing them back in his pocket. Clive raised his eyebrows.

"If you say so Sam."

"It's just temporary Clive, that's all. 'Till I get this leg sorted."

"I get it Sam, it was similar for me," said Clive unloading some glasses from the glass washing machine. Sam put down his glass and looked at Clive.

"For me it was purely booze, and my problem wasn't a physical one. It was emotional pain," said Clive, "my wife left me." Clive laughed but not in a humorous way. "That's not quite accurate. She left me because of the booze. I was already in trouble, drank too much. I just used her leaving me as an excuse to drink more."

"You're the second person today giving me

the gypsy's warning about my leg and the booze."

"Sorry Sam, didn't mean to intrude."

"No worries, Clive. I've known you what, five, six years now and never seen you take a sip of booze. Always assumed you'd always been tee-total."

"The opposite Sam, I'm a drunk, a lifelong drunk, which is why I can't take a sip. Don't get me wrong Sam, I'm not preaching against booze. Be funny if I was, running this bar 'n all. Nothing I'd love more than a cold beer on a hot sunny day. But one beer and the door to hell opens up for me."

"Well, I never," said Sam "How'd you kick it.?"

"Twelve step program, lifelong member. Another?" Sam nodded a yes. Clive poured a generous double Ten High bourbon. "Those pills though, they're more addictive than booze I've heard." Randazzo scratched his ear in a distracted way.

"Yeah, well maybe, but like I say, it's just temporary."

The detective was careful driving home. He could always pull rank if he got pulled over, but it wasn't a good look for a senior detective. He thought about what Frankie and Clive had said. He hadn't been entirely truthful when he told Clive it was all about his leg. Some of it was but some of it wasn't. It wasn't the whole picture. Since the kids had left home to go to college upstate, his relationship with his wife Martha had deteriorated a bit. Then the shooting and the constant leg pain. He knew opioids were potentially addictive *but not for guys like me. I can stop whenever I want to..*

Martha also seemed to complain a lot more about his working long hours these days. *Probably 'cos she hadn't got the kids to look after and distract her? Maybe I should take her out for dinner> We haven't done that in a while.* He resolved to suggest that as soon as he got home, but Martha had left a note saying she'd gone to see her friend Ruth and she'd prepared some cold cuts for his supper and left them in the fridge. *I'll suggest the dinner as soon as she gets back.*

By the time Martha returned home, Randazzo was fast asleep in his chair, snoring like a pig. Martha threw a cover over him and went to bed.

Martha tossed and turned in her bed, unable to sleep. She couldn't get over the change in her husband since he'd been shot in the leg. The English guy Frankie had saved Sam's life, but she sometimes wondered. The man she'd known before seemed different, as though something in Sam had died that day. She got up and found the old photograph albums, the ones they used to put actual pictures in before the advent of digital.

Leafing through the albums, she variously laughed and cried as the pictures brought back all the happy memories. They had some hard times in the past she knew, but they were happy hard times. Sam had done well in his career, rising in the ranks from traffic cop to Lieutenant Detective. They had two wonderful children who were hopefully on their own path to a fulfilling adulthood. The bedroom door opened.

"You're still awake?" said Randazzo. Martha looked at him steadily, residual tears in her eyes. "Sorry, dumb question, of course you are. Are those what I think they are?" he said looking at the albums strewn over the counterpane. Martha didn't reply. Randazzo wandered over to the other side of the bed, sat down, picked up one of the albums and flipped the pages slowly. "Good times," he said, "I remember those."

CHAPTER 14

PRESENT

Friday 21 February 2020
Frankie & Son?

Frankie emailed the picture and his requirements to Gareth, the once wayward genius IT expert they employed. Gareth was Frankie's business partner's nephew, so Barnsie had left it to Frankie to make the decision to take him on or not. He'd approved it and it had proved to be a good decision. Not only had Gareth improved their own internal IT systems, but his skills had meant they were able to create a new division, offering cyber security services to their existing clients and to sell cyber security services to a whole new range of clientele.

After sending the picture to Gareth, Frankie sat down in the lanai and gazed over the bay, trying to assemble his thoughts. Just as he sat down, his computer pinged to signal a new email. He got up and looked at his messages. It was an email from someone called Ross, marked strictly confidential. On further inspection Frankie saw it was from the Naples Police Dept and had an attachment. He read the body of the email.

Mr. Armstrong, Detective Randazzo asked me to forward this directly to you. Detective Randazzo said he only wanted to know of any phone activity from two months prior to a certain date. He said you'd know why. If you want phone numbers for any prior period, please let me know.
Ross Beaumont Naples Police IT Dept.

Frankie moved the excel document to his desktop and opened it. It contained a list of phone numbers taken from Sean Kennedy's cell phone with associated names from Sean's contact list. Other numbers without any identity were also listed. The list showed all calls made and received in time and date order. Frankie printed the list off and began to examine it.

He got a red marker pen, walked over to his dining table in the main room of the condo, put the list down on the table and looked at it. He thought about it and decided that three weeks prior to the Hurricane, should be enough lead time to find the information he required. If Sean had been employed, subsequent to the hurricane, then any relevant calls should be immediately after Irma had struck. The detective said it was not long after Hurricane Irma, that the Kennedy family began to live a life of relative luxury and that Roman Plaza was the most likely place in his opinion.

Frankie began to eliminate those numbers that he could identify as members of Sean's family or names that were obviously not work related, such as Ace Hardware or Boatyard etc. By such method he reduced the list down to a manageable number of phone numbers.

He grabbed his cell and was about to start calling the numbers in order when his doorbell chimed. He opened it and there stood the young man he'd talked briefly to at the pool.

"Hello, remember me?" the young man said with an uncertain look on his face.

"I do, said Frankie, "we spoke briefly at the pool the other day, is there something I can help you with?" The boy looked uncomfortable and awkward.

"Erm..., would it be possible to come in?"

Frankie was a little taken aback, but quickly assessed the situation. The young man didn't seem threatening or desperate, more of a boy really. And Frankie could handle himself. He reckoned this young man didn't represent any kind of real threat, so he opened the door wide. The young man hesitated then entered the apartment and looked around then back at Frankie. Frankie closed the door, then turned to face the young man.

"Sorry about this, but may I sit down?"

"Yes sure," said Frankie and gestured to a chair at the dining table. Frankie remained standing. Charlie immediately came to sniff at the boy's leg. The young man, who had been looking down at his hands, now bent over a little and lowered one hand to ruffle the fur on Charlie's head. Charlie responded by licking the boy's hand.

"Sorry about Charlie, he thinks everyone's his friend."

"No worries," said the boy "I like dogs. He's really nice." Frankie waited. The boy stopped petting Charlie, looked up at Frankie and spoke.

"My name's Aaron and I...," the boy hesitated then looked Frankie straight in the eye. "I think you're my... No.., sorry, I know you're my father." The boy said with certainty.

"I'm what!" said Frankie and sat down. Charlie came to sit at his feet.

"I know, said Aaron, "I guess it's a shock, a lot to take in, but I didn't know how else to say it. I'm sorry if I'm causing you stress but..."

Frankie was beginning to recover.

"I don't understand..."

"You remember Hana?"

"Oh..." said Frankie, the memories flooding back.

CHAPTER 15

BEFORE

2003 - Iraq Frankie and Hana

"You're funny," Hana said when they first met. She was helping out as a nurse, attending to the mostly badly wounded soldiers. A bombed out Iraqi soldier's barracks had been adapted to serve as a makeshift hospital. The walls were solid enough and the make shift roof formed from canvas. Beds were lined up along either side of the pockmarked walls. It was crude but adequate. Frankie had suffered a shrapnel wound to his leg and although not serious in itself, it had become infected. The army doctor had diagnosed the early stages of sepsis so Frankie had been hospitalized so they could administer the necessary drugs to halt the infection.

"Funny how?" asked Frankie.

"Your accent and your looks."

"Well thanks a bunch," said Frankie feigning hurt. She tucked in the bed sheets and Frankie watched her every move. He'd known as soon as he'd set eyes on her that something special had happened. He was attracted to her in a way that he'd never experienced before.

"No, I didn't mean it like that. I meant you're different that's all. In a nice way."

The following day Frankie waited anxiously for sight of Hana. He was able to get up and move around now but was told not to overdo it. The morning dragged with no sight of Hana. After lunch, he was dozing in his bed when she came to see how he was.

"So, how come you speak such good English," Frankie asked, "and how come you're allowed to look after a British soldier. Isn't that against your religion or whatever?"

"Well, the answer to your first question is that we had an English teacher in the school I attended." Frankie raised his eyebrows. "I'm Kurdish, a Kurdish Christian. And I'm probably hated by Saddam as much as he hates you."

"What's your name?" asked Frankie.

"Hana, it means hope. Yours?"

"Francis. I believe it means free man."

"Well, there we are then," she said, "we have hope and freedom."

"Sound good together, don't they?" said Frankie looking her straight in the eye. She looked a little embarrassed but smiled and said,

"I think so too."

"Erm, excuse me for asking er.. Hana. And tell me to mind my own business if you want…, but are you married or anything?"

"No, I'm not married…, or anything, as you put it."

At that moment, Frankie breathed out a sigh of relief. He knew he was totally head over heels in love with Hana. Knew it like he'd never been so certain of anything else in his whole life.

"You should be okay by tomorrow the doctor said. Now we've pumped you full of these drugs. Your wound wasn't that badly infected, so I think your doctor was being a bit over cautious. Better safe than sorry though with sepsis. So, you'll be on your way back to your regiment soon enough?"

Frankie knew he had to act quickly.

"Listen Hana, I know this sounds crazy, but…" He ran out of words, trying to find a way of asking without blowing it.

"Go on," she said in a way that he thought might have been encouragement.

"Do you…? Listen I know we've only known each other two days, not even that, but…"

"Yes, I feel something, if that's what you're asking. But these situations can, I don't know, make people emotional. Feelings get exaggerated."

"You're right of course, they do," he replied, "but even so, I have to tell you that I've never felt like this before. And I don't think it's the situation. I know how crazy that sounds. Can we find a way of seeing each other again?"

"Well, this hospital is going to be here a while, unless it gets bombed of course. But the fighting is a long way to the west of here, so if you can get back here sometime, maybe we can meet up again."

CHAPTER 16

PRESENT

Friday 21February 2020
Frankie & son

"Yes, of course I remember Hana. Are you saying....is she still, still alive? Is she over here?" Frankie felt dizzy and had to stop talking. Aaron looked away then faced Frankie.

"My mother Hana was killed, two years after you left. She was killed in a roadside bomb explosion in Basra, near where you were stationed during the war."

Frankie was stunned, and speechless for a while, then he found his voice.

"And how do you know about...?"

"About you?" Aaron finished Frankie's sentence for him.

"Yes, about me."

"My mother kept a diary. I was brought up by her sister Naza. When I was old enough to start asking about why I had no father, she explained to me about my mother falling in love with a British soldier. I didn't really understand then but when I got a bit older, she gave me my mother's diary to read."

"I tried to contact Hana when I knew we were going back home to the UK," said Frankie, but I couldn't find her. The hospital had been bombed. When I got there was nothing left, just rubble. I searched and searched. I tried every way I knew how to find her. In the end I concluded she'd been killed in the attack on the hospital. We'd agreed to keep our relationship a secret. I said I'd find a way of getting her back to the UK. We were going to get married, but we knew it wouldn't be straightforward. There were many obstacles in the way, but I was determined to get her back to England. Hana was the love of my life, still is. I'm finding this all very hard to take in Aaron."

"I understand, but from what my sister told me, my mother only ever had the one relationship." Frankie nodded.

"How come you were able to get into the States?" asked Frankie.

"I live here now. I did well at school and there was a scheme run by some American organization that sort of focused on war orphans and organized for some of them to go to America. To try and make some sort of recompense, I guess. I don't know, but I applied, and was lucky. I was fostered by a really nice family. It was supposed to be temporary, but I'm still living there."

"And what did you tell the people, your foster parents I suppose, where did you tell them you were going when you decided to come to meet me?"

"I told them a mixture of truth and fibs, stretched the truth a bit so they'd let me come. Told them I might have found my real father. Told them it wasn't definite but that I'd talked to you on the phone, and you'd said you'd be happy to talk to me if I came to see you. I showed them the newspaper cuttings I'd saved, about the woman being attacked by the shark last year and your involvement and so on, so I knew about you and this place. That this was where you might be living now. I had money saved up, so I could easily afford the air ticket and a couple of nights in a cheap hotel. So, I came down here. You know the rest."

"What about school. I assume you go to school. You'll be what, 16 or 17 I guess?" said Frankie doing the math."

"Yeah, I'm sixteen and a half and I'm in 10th Grade. At a really good school. Speaking of which, I have to be back there tomorrow. My flight leaves tonight from Fort Myers. That's why I came to see you today. I knew I had to pluck up the courage. If I'd left without telling you I don't think I could have come back again, and my trip would have been for nothing."

"And how did you find me?"

"Obviously, I looked on the internet but couldn't find anything definite, then I read about you in the papers. When you found that murderer and got shot in the head. They gave some of your personal history, including that you'd been a soldier and served in Iraq. I went from there really."

"Yes, the media couldn't get enough of it. The alligator attack gave them some great headlines. I tried to minimize the publicity, but they wouldn't let go."

"May I ask you how you came to live in Florida?"

"It's a long story, but during the Iraq war, a US soldier saved my life. A guy called Joe Nelson. I promised him that if he ever needed my help with anything in the future, 'I'd be more than happy pay back the favor. When I left the army, I kind of forgot all about it, but Joe contacted me in the UK and asked me to come over here to help him find his missing nephew. I'll maybe get to tell you the full story sometime. But it all worked out. Once I got here, I got to really like Naples and somehow, in the process of helping Joe, I inherited his nephew's dog, Charlie here."

"I really look forward to hearing all about it, but I have to go now." Aaron stood and so did Frankie. "I have an Uber waiting outside. Got to go now, I'll miss my flight. It was.... good to finally meet you."

"Likewise," said Frankie. "Listen, I have so

many questions. I'm still taking all this in."

"I understand," said Aaron and stuck out his hand to shake. Frankie took his hand in his then pulled the boy close. They held each other for a few moments, then stood apart.

"I loved your Hana. Loved her like I've never loved anyone since."

"Yes, I think I knew that from reading her diary. My contact details are in the envelope as well, so feel free to call or email whatever, anytime. Maybe we can get to know each other" Frankie looked at the envelope.

"I will," he said.

CHAPTER 17

PRESENT

Friday 21February 2020
Frankie & Daisy

They were sitting at one of the small two people high tables in Cibao, Frankie's favorite restaurant. Frankie told her about Aaron's visit and his revelations. She listened, incredulity written on her face

"I'm finding this just so... so hard to take in. You have a grown-up son!" She took a sip of her martini.

"That's what he claims."

"You doubt it then."

"Yes, I doubt it."

"Oh," said Daisy taking another sip of her martini. "Frankie told her about his romance with Hana in Iraq but tuned down the intensity of his feelings for Hana.

"So surely, it's possible he is your son then?"

"Not medically possible, no."

"Oh," said Daisy "Did you ever tell your wife

Penny? Did you ever tell her about Hana?"

"No. I was so upset when I couldn't find Hana. I assumed she was dead, killed when the hospital was destroyed. The only way I could cope was to try to put her out of my mind completely. It was just too painful to remember. Marrying Penny when I left the army might well have been part of my way of putting it all behind me. And maybe Penny sensed there was something not quite right. After all she did leave me, twice."

"Yup," said Daisy. "Woman's intuition."

*

Frankie had met and dated his future wife Penny before he decided to join the army. They'd met when he made up a foursome to do a pal a favor. They were well suited, and everyone expected them to get married. But Frankie was restless and fed up with his dead-end job, so one drunken night, he and his best friend Derek Barns, or Barnsie as everyone called him, decided to join the army. Both Derek and Frankie enjoyed army life, until they were sent to Iraq. That changed everything.

Frankie had proposed to Penny within three months of getting back from Iraq and leaving the army. She accepted and they were married. It was a small wedding, by contemporary standards back then. Frankie's Derek *Barnsie* was best man. They'd chosen to have the wedding ceremony in a quaint church out in the Cheshire countryside, followed by a meal in a "gourmet" pub. There were only forty guests or so, but that's how Penny had wanted it.

After they'd returned from their honeymoon in Mallorca, Penny went back to her job, teaching in a local primary school and Frankie set about getting a job.

Nothing appealed to Frankie. Iraq had somehow dulled his ambition.

"What about going back to the building trade?" Penny had asked him.

"Yeah, but I got bored with the building game, said Frankie, "which is why I joined the army. Same with Barnsie, he was bored with his job, and the army was his way out as well. And we both enjoyed it, until they sent us to fight in Iraq. I mean how unfair was that, sending soldiers to fight a war?"

"You need to do something Frankie Armstrong. The man I married wouldn't sit around all day. The Frankie I married would be up and at 'em. Do you think you might be suffering some PTS?"

"Don't be silly. Listen, I'll give the job thing some serious thought, but right now I'm off to the pub. Said I'd meet Derek for a pint. Don't wait up." He kissed Penny on the cheek and left.

As he walked to the pub, he thought about what Penny had just said. He knew she'd been patient, appreciating the way the war had affected him, although she didn't know the whole story. He didn’t see any point in telling her about Hana. As for PTS, *what a ridiculous thing to say* Frankie laughed out loud, a scoffing laugh as walked along, but inside knew she wasn’t far off the mark.

Apart from Penny, the occasional chat with his younger brother, his only other meaningful contact was with his old pal and fellow soldier Barnsie. He met Barnsie for a drink in the pub most Friday evenings. This Friday evening would be a game changer.

“How long we been out of the army now Frankie?”

“Just over a year, I guess.”

“You still haven’t found anything you want to do?”

“Nope, just can’t find anything that appeals. You?

“The same, but I’ve had an idea. We’re in good shape, fit, capable, and in my case, extremely handsome.”

“Have you been to the opticians lately? Frankie said, then continued. “So, what’s the idea, Hollywood? You always did fancy being an actor even as a kid, soppy git.”

“Nah, Hollywood comes later, Security.”

“You want to elaborate on that?” Frankie asked.

“You know, we talked about it the other week, having our own firm. We even had the name,

A&B Security Services."

"I seem to remember that was after several pints of Groves Bitter."

"Well, I don't know about you, but I was serious. What we needed was a bit of luck to get started," said Derek.

"Okay, and so...?"

"Well, remember Malcolm, posh lad who never really fitted in at school?" asked Derek.

"I do, yes, Malcolm White, glasses, clever bugger. Wasn't there long. His folks moved him to another school if I remember right. Just as well, he was always being picked on, poor sod."

"You got him. Well, he isn't a poor sod anymore. Quite a rich sod in fact. I bumped into him in Manchester. Didn't recognize him but he remembered me. I was having a pizza with Rita and he comes over. It's Derek isn't, remember me? he says. Anyway, once he said his name I did. And you know what, he remembered me sticking up for him a couple of times? Saved him from a beating from that well-known dickhead and shit for brains Bonzo, remember Brian Onslow?"

"I remember," said Frankie, "go on. I assume there's a happy outcome from this chance meeting?" There was. Malcolm gave them their first assignment and they were off and running.

*

"Listen, I'm sorry about earlier. I was an arsehole." Frankie said when he got back that evening. Penny looked at him and stood up.

"I'm going to bed now. Apology accepted, but don't think that's going to get you into my knickers tonight. No sex for a month, make that six weeks."

"Six weeks? Supposing I told you I'd got a job, could you shorten the punishment period to say, what, half an hour?"

"How could you have got a job while you were drinking with Barnsie in the pub? You going to be a barman, is that it? 'cos if it is, the ban has just been extended to three months minimum."

"I'm going into the security business" Frankie said. It was the first time she'd seen him excited about anything for a long time.

"Security" what kind of job's that?" she'd asked. "Sounds worse than being a barman, what, doorman at some sleazy club?"

"Exactly that, in fact, a strip club, keeping the riff-raff out and protecting all those vulnerable, naked women."

"In your dreams Frankie Armstrong, be serious. What are you going to do to keep me in the style I'm accustomed to? Scratch that, to keep me in the style I'd like to get accustomed to?"

"I am serious. I'm going into business with Barnsie. A&B Security services."

"What, you and Derek Barnes going into business, doing what kind of security exactly?"

"The kind that pays a lot. We've already got our first job. Barnsie bumped into an old school friend. Big knob in a merchant bank now and they've got a Saudi prince, some rich Arab guy coming to Manchester, well somewhere near Preston ultimately, visiting some racing stables to buy a horse he said."

"Barnsie's got friends like that, since when?"

"It's a long story, but we're doing it. What's to lose?"

"Well, I suppose when you look at it like that. But this Saudi whatever person, surely he'll have his own security people?"

"Yeah, but they want some local support, and that's us." Three grand for two days work."

"Isn't that sort of work a bit...dangerous Frankie? What if people take the opportunity to attack him while he's away from his own country? Those sorts of filthy rich people always have lots of enemies."

"Don't you worry, we're more than a match for anyone. Do I look like a pushover?" Penny looked at him, just under six-foot tall, dark brown hair, crooked nose from a scrap he'd had with an army mate when they were both a bit drunk.

"No Frankie you don't look like a pushover. So, tell me more about this crazy idea."

"It's not crazy. I'm as fit as I was in the army, fitter probably, and Barnsie, you wouldn't want to tangle with him. He could probably give the Karate Kid lessons. And this contract is only the start. Barnsie's mate says there's plenty more work if we do okay with this one."

"You'd better get a new suit then," said Penny,

and smiled.

"What about the ban?"

"Hmm, I'll consider a temporary suspension," she said and laughed. Frankie chased her upstairs.

*

A few years later A&B Security Services had expanded its range of services to include professional investigations, alarm monitoring and response, key holding, safe deposit boxes, credit checking, security guarding for business, twenty-four-hour CCTV Monitoring, personal security guards, then with the help of Barnsie's genius IT nerdy nephew, they moved into cyber security.

CHAPTER 18

Friday 21 February 2020
Frankie & Daisy evening continued

Frankie was suddenly aware of Daisy speaking.

"Frankie...are you listening to me? I don't think you heard a word I've just said, have you?"

"Sorry," said Frankie, I was miles away."

"Yes, I think I could see that." Daisy frowned and took a drink of her martini.

"I was asking what's he like, this boy who claims he's your son?"

"Well, I don't really know do I, but on first acquaintance, he seems like a really nice guy, the sort of son any father might be proud of."

"Hmm, so why do you think he's claiming you're his father?"

"No idea Daisy. Still trying to make sense of it. Look, let's leave it for now."

"Okay Frankie, I understand, but any developments..."

"You'll be the first to know," said Frankie smiling.

"So, change of subject. How's the mystery jewels investigation going? Made any progress?"

"Sort of, but I have a confession to make."

"Really. What have you been up to Frankie?"

You know Randazzo asked me to gather info about what happened when Irma hit Naples and more specifically how the floods affected the Roman Plaza condo?"

"I do, so?"

"So, I went to visit Roman Plaza and I told the guy there I was gathering information on behalf of my significant other, the one and only famous Daisy Scoop Metcalf, journalist."

"You really said that?"

"Well, other than the words famous and scoop, yeah."

"That'll cost you buster. I don't just let anyone say they're working for me. I have my reputation to consider." Frankie smiled.

"Would another martini be sufficient payment?"

"Call it part payment. I'll work out what else I need from you later."

"Deal," said Frankie raising his glass and laughing.

"So come on smart pants, what have you found out so far?"

"Well, I've narrowed things down a bit. I called all the numbers that Sean Kennedy either made or received on his cell around the time in question. Sean had been working on some private properties, houses and flats, but the people who owned those houses or apartments wouldn't leave such a valuable item around for the workman to find would they? Anyway, long story short, I found the guy who employed Sean to work on the condos at Roman Plaza. So, it looks as if Randazzo could be right. Sean's job was to rip out all the sheetrock walls and completely reconstruct them. In the process, maybe he came across the jewels. Maybe it they were hidden behind a wall, or something? Wouldn't be difficult, the way you Americans construct interior walls, would it?"

"I suppose not, but why him?"

"Two reasons, one he was the sheetrock specialist, and his job was to rip out all the walls in the ground floor condos with a view to reconstructing them once the places were dried out. And..., Randazzo said Sean Kennedy had form. Sometimes stuff was reported missing after he'd worked in a place. But Randazzo couldn't find any record of him being prosecuted for theft. He was investigated, but it seems the items in question were never ones of great value, and nothing was ever proven. On the other hand, the people I spoke to that employed him, said he was really good at his job. Could do the work in much less time than most, so maybe he was cut a bit of slack?"

"Next obvious question then is, who had the jewelry hidden in their condo or wherever?"

said Daisy.

"I don't know. I need to go back to Roman Plaza and talk to the manager, see if I can get a bit more information. The ground floor condos were all damaged and like I said, everything had to be ripped out, kitchen, walls ceiling everything. The people around the pool told me there are ten condos at ground floor level. Apparently, only two of the residents weren't there at the time the damage occurred."

"So?"

"Well, it stands to reason that the residents who were there at the time, wouldn't leave anything valuable for the workmen to find, so if Sean found the jewels hidden in any of the condos at Roman Plaza, it has to be one of the condos where the owners were absent at the time of the flood and the subsequent ripping out of the insides. Does that make sense?"

"Perfect sense," said Daisy. "But how are you going to find out who they were? I don't see how you're going to maintain the 'gathering hurricane data for Scoop Metcalf' story though," daisy said using air quotes. "Who was there and not there at the time of the flood, wouldn't be pertinent to that, would it?"

"Yeah I realize that. I'll have to think up another angle"

"Well, while you're thinking," said Daisy nodding to her empty cocktail glass.

"Sorry, getting distracted." Frankie managed to get the attention of a waitress and asked for another gin martini and another beer. "So, going back to Mr. Kennedy and what happened to the jewels he had hidden away at his home. Randazzo thinks it's possible, more than possible maybe, that Sean Kennedy was killed to get the jewelry back. The jewelry went missing from Kennedy's house and he died or was killed, probably by the person taking what they considered was their property, although it might not have been their property, strictly speaking? Sean's death and the jewels going missing from his house is a big coincidence, and Sam doesn't like coincidences."

"Maybe his wife took it and sold it, pawned it or something, or maybe Sean Kennedy was killed for something unconnected, and his son took the opportunity to take the jewelry and dispose of it.?"

"Or his daughter? Come on… let's have some gender equality here…"

"Okay, or his daughter," said Daisy smiling. "Or maybe the poor guy just died of natural causes? What did the autopsy say was the cause of death?"

"Inconclusive. But more than likely he died from natural causes, a heart attack."

"Well, there you are," said Daisy taking a sip of her martini.

"They did find some heart irregularities that might have been pertinent, but no clear indication of why it happened at that time. And the report noted that he had a huge amount of alcohol in his system, which could also have been a contributory factor."

"And is it possible to fake a heart attack?"

"Not really sure," answered Frankie, "I'm going to look into it some more, but I seem to remember reading that an injection of potassium chloride can cause heart failure but can look like a heart attack on an autopsy. There's always the good old pillow or a plastic bag method, but that can usually be detected, not always. But maybe if you're looking for it?" Their first course came. Frankie was having a lettuce wedge with blue cheese sauce and Daisy, crab cakes.

"Those look delicious," said Frankie.

"Yeah, well if you want to keep all your fingers, I advise you to keep your hands off them buddy," came the reply. They both tucked in.

CHAPTER 19

PRESENT

Saturday 22 February 2020
The jewelry identified.

An email from Gareth the following day was very illuminating. After reading through it and looking at the enhanced pictures of the jewelry, Frankie felt the thrill of excitement pass thought him. *Progress.* He reached for his cell and called Randazzo after four rings, an automated message kicked in,

"I'm unavailable until Monday. A rare weekend off. If it's an urgent matter please call 239-213-4844, otherwise please leave a message and I'll get back to you Monday. Have a great weekend." Frankie left a message.

"Hi Sam, Frankie here. Weekend off, wow! Cushy job. Nothing urgent but I have something on the jewelry. You'll like it... I think. Call me as soon as. Hope you have a relaxing weekend. Speak Monday." Frankie went to make a coffee, then went back to his PC and read through Gareth's email once more and looked at the pictures again. Then he clicked on the link Gareth had provided. It took him to a page where the theft of the jewelry was laid out in detail. Frankie read... Sir Arthur Vicars was the Ulster King of Arms at Dublin Castle, and amongst other duties, was responsible for protecting the Crown Jewels of Ireland. The State Jewels of Ireland were not made for the real King of Ireland, the last native Irish King being Rory O'Connor, who died 1198.

The Crown Jewels of Ireland, worth an estimated $1,500 (approx. $20m in today's money), comprised a heavily jeweled star and badge regalia originally created in 1831 for the Sovereign and Grand Master of the Order of St. Patrick, an order of knighthood established in 1783 by King George III.

***

Dublin Ireland 1907

"Pour me another one would you Pierce? I'm just getting the taste."

"Yes, Sir Arthur. Will the others be joining us?

"What? oh yes, we shall have a party to celebrate erm... well I'll think of something to celebrate once I've had a few more of these." The door to his chambers opened, and in strode Francis Shackleton, Sir Arthur's SIC and brother of the great intrepid explorer Ernest Shackleton

"Is that that you Francis?" asked Sir Arthur, now spifflicated.

"Yes, Sir Arthur, 'tis me indeed."

"Er, help yourself Francis, don't know where that damn Pierce has got to." Shackleton helped himself to a large one and sat down. He took a big gulp of Irish whisky.

"Anyone else coming tonight?"

"Oh yes, quite a few more to arrive yet. I've invited your friend Richard and that Francis Bennett Goldney character. He said he'd bring along one or two ladies. We'll have a bit of a hooley, some music and who knows what else?" Shackleton smiled a wicked smile.

"Shaping up to be one of those nights, is it?"

"I certainly hope so," said Sir Arthur gulping the rest of his drink down in one "Pour me another old chap would you?"

*

The next morning, Sir Arthur had the mother and father of a hangover. He stumbled through the room where the main 'festivities' had occurred. There were clothes strewn about, a couple of people still asleep on the floor. Drinking vessels variously scattered on tables and the floor. Sir Arthur found one on a table, half full. He smelled it.

"Hair of the dog." He said and gulped it down. "Ahh, sweet Jesus, Joseph and Mary," he exclaimed and breathed out a deep sigh. Took another sip, then drank the rest. He stood for a moment, letting the alcohol do its job. Feeling a little more human, he decided he'd better carry out his duties and check the strong room in the tower. He felt about his person searching for the keys. He couldn't find them at first, but then with a sigh of relief, spotted them lying on the table by the chair he'd occupied the previous evening. Picking the keys up, he made his way to the tower.

Climbing the stairs slowly he reached the landing and fumbled with the keys, finding the one for the library door. He opened it and went inside. The guards would have made their regular rounds so all should be well, *but what the devil were my keys doing on that table?* Walking over to the safe containing the crown jewels, he found the key, inserted it and opened the safe door. The safe was empty.

His legs lost all their strength and he collapsed on the floor. A few seconds later he recovered consciousness. Slowly, with the help of a nearby chair he stood. His hangover had returned a hundredfold. He slowly made his way to the door of the strongroom where the rest of the treasures were stored. The safe holding the jewels should have been in the strongroom, but when it had arrived at the castle it was found to be too big to pass through the strong room doors, hence it remained in the library and vulnerable.

Sir Arthur opened the strongroom and saw

the Sword of State still in its place, along with the maces. The manuscripts also seemed to have been left untouched He sighed again... *thank the Lord for small mercies.* Then, as the enormity of the loss began to filter into his brain, he began to imagine the punishment he would suffer for being responsible for the loss the Crown Jewels. He soiled his trousers.

CHAPTER 20

PRESENT

Later, Saturday 22 February 2020
Back to Roman Plaza

Frankie spent some time trying to concoct a story that would enable him to get the information he wanted from the manager at Roman Plaza but could only think of one approach *when all else fails, just tell the truth…Could do with calling Mike Lee first, but as I don't have his number, just have to hope he's there….* Frankie set off from Acadiana for the ten-minute walk to Roman Plaza. He walked around the back towards the pool are and as he turned the corner of the building, nearly bumped into Mike Lee. Mike Lee started to apologize, then recognized Frankie.

"Hey, you're the guy that was here the other day, the reporter's friend."

"That's me, Frankie Armstrong."

"You want to go talk to the pool crowd again? They're probably all there. Where else would you be on a day like today, other than by the pool or on the beach?"

"Yeah, tough choice," said Frankie smiling, "but actually It's you I want to talk to if you have time."

"Well, I was just leaving. I'm not usually here Saturday afternoon, but I forgot my iPad. Damn devices, life was so much better before all this technology crap." He looked at his watch. "I guess I have ten minutes, but no more. I have to meet my wife at Waterside, shopping." He raised his eyes to heaven. "Let's go sit over there," he said pointing at a little wooden table with four chairs around it. They walked over and sat down. "Okay, shoot," he said.

Frankie said what he was about to tell him was confidential, so he hoped he could rely on his discretion.

"You can," replied Mike Lee. Frankie proceeded to explain about the jewels, not everything, but enough to justify the questions he wanted to ask. "So, the story you told me before wasn't true?"

"Partly. My girlfriend is Daisy Metcalf, and she is a reporter. But the gathering information for her was a bit of a white lie." Mike Lee rubbed his chin.

"But this story about the missing jewelry is on the level. And you're asking these questions on behalf of this detective Randazzo, did you say?"

"Yes, and you can call the Naples Police department and check me out with him. You can do that now, but I don't know if he'll be in." Mike lee looked at him and paused, then spoke.

"No, its not necessary. After we met the other day, I checked you out with the folks at Acadiana and they said you were okay. So, what is it you want to know?"

"When I spoke with the people in the pool, they said that there were two people who owned ground floor condos, that weren't here at the time of the flood and that they were both angry that you'd had their condos torn apart without their permission."

"That's about right, yeah."

"We think that this guy Kennedy, who did the work on your grand floor condos, ripping them out and so on, we think he might have found the jewels hidden somewhere in one of the condos. It seems unlikely that any of the people who were here at the time would have left anything valuable for him to steal, so if they were taken from here, which is a possibility, then it had to be from one of the absent owner's units."

"Got it," said Mike Lee. "So, you want to know who those owners are and all the information I can give you on them?" Frankie said nothing while Mike Lee thought it through "I'm not sure about this, I mean, am I breaching confidences here?"

"I'm not asking for anything confidential and nothing that the police couldn't get anyway, but they would be much more intrusive. All I want are details of who they are, and which are their units, plus where their main homes are. And, if you know, what they do for a living, if they're still working that is." Mike rubbed his chin again.

"Well, like you say, nothing the cops couldn't get if they wanted. And I guess it wouldn't be good to have the cops poking their noses in around here. Not that anyone has anything to hide, but folks get spooked by cops asking questions. Listen, write down your email address and I'll email you later with all the information you've asked for. If I don't go now, I'll be in big trouble with the boss."

"Thanks," said Frankie and gave Mike a business card.

"And you don't say where you got this information from okay? I'm still not entirely sure I'm doing the right thing?"

"I promise Mike, no one will know," said Frankie. "By the way, are either of them here now?"

"I think they're both here, but Otto and his wife like to go cruising so they could be away for a few days, I don't know. Brandon Mellor's definitely here, but he pretty well keeps himself to himself these days, ever since his wife died. Poor woman, killed by an intruder at their home in the UK. Such a tragedy, she was one very classy lady."

"Okay, well thanks Mike," said Frankie. They both stood up, shook hands and left.

*

The following morning was Sunday and Frankie decided to make it a day of rest. Fishing, and sunbathing on the beach or round the pool catching up on the latest gossip, with the odd beer thrown in. Daisy was away on some assignment, so he was on his own for the rest of the weekend. Mid-morning, he received an email from Mike Lee. It had little in the way of preamble and simply provided the information Frankie had asked for. It said...

Frankie

Two ground floor unit owners were absent at the time of the flood. Unit Five was owned by a British couple Brandon and the late Fiona Mellor who live in Virginia Water Surry. Brandon is some sort of investment broker. Unit six is owned by a German couple Otto and Hildegard Kellerman. They live somewhere near Munich, I think. Otto is an art dealer and owns an art gallery somewhere over here.

These were the only two ground floor condo owners who weren't occupying their condos at the time. All the rest of the ground floor condos were occupied, seven of them with permanent residents and one other one, which the overseas owners happened to be staying in at the time of the flood.

Frankie read the email and replied to Mike, thanking him for the information. He also asked Mike if he would be kind enough to email him when Otto Kellerman was back in residence, *maybe that's pushing it a bit?* Thought Frankie. He waited a few minutes to see if Mike Lee responded, but nothing. He shrugged *you don't ask you don't get.* He just hoped he hadn't pushed Mike into closing down any further cooperation.

He turned his mind to choosing what to do. The tide table seemed a good place to start, high tide being something to take into account when choosing what time to go fishing. 2:00 p.m. was high tide so he decided on a trip down to the beach to get some sunbathing and a swim in first, then off to the pier for some fishing.

CHAPTER 21

PRESENT

Monday 24 February 2020
Frankie and Brandon Mellor

The IT genius Gareth's email had astounded Frankie. And once more Frankie thought how close they'd come to not employing him and thanked the Lord they had. Gareth had been the archetypal layabout, moody and uncooperative. Thankfully, Frankie had seen the glimmer of something in Gareth. Something that made him curious enough to talk to the boy, to give him a chance to open up. He soon discovered that the boy was incredibly shy and was attempting to cover it up by appearing belligerent.

Once Frankie had prised him out of his protective shell, he found Gareth to be quite witty and pleasant to talk to. He also sensed the latent intelligence and IT skills, which up to then Gareth had employed hacking into systems for fun and to show off. In offering Gareth a job, Frankie had taken a big chance, and made it clear to Gareth he'd done so. Gareth responded positively and once he found his confidence, he was unstoppable.

Using the information provided by Gareth, Frankie spent the rest of the morning doing some more research on the jewels. It had been productive, and he couldn't wait to tell Randazzo what he'd manage to discover. His cell buzzed. He looked at the screen and answered.

"Hi Sam, glad you called, I have some quite interesting news. You're going to love this."

"Go ahead Frankie I'm all ears."

"I asked my man in the UK to enhance the image of the jewelry, which he did. But he also went a step further and used some sort of sophisticated image matching software. He's pretty sure, and so am I now, that these are the Irish Crown Jewels which went missing in 1907. Stolen from Dublin Castle."

"Madonna Mia!" exclaimed Randazzo. "You sure?"

"The images match so there's little doubt it's true. Could be copies I suppose but you said they looked like the real thing."

"I'm no real expert, but they certainly looked genuine. Does anyone else know about this?"

"Only Gareth, the guy who did the imaging and matching. I've already told him this is an ultra-confidential matter. I will tell my business partner Barnsie. We don't keep secrets from each other about anything. But he's discreet and won't breathe a word to anyone either."

"Good, I need to think what implications this may have, so let's keep shtum, keep it to ourselves for now, okay? It doesn't prevent us from pursuing the investigation of the theft, we just don't mention the Irish connection?"

"Okay Sam, mum's the word. Does this mean you won't be going formal with this, you still want me to carry on investigating under the radar?"

"Yeah, I think that would be best. I give it to the department, and pretty soon, some bright spark would find out the Irish angle and that would be that. I have no doubt it would be taken out of my hands. I'm going to have to ask you to bear with me on this Frankie. Are you okay to be in this for the long run? I'll find some way to compensate you."

"Yes Sam, I'm hooked. I'd be reluctant to let go now it's getting really interesting."

"Great, who knows Frankie, we recover the jewels and there could well be a nice reward. I mean you're the one who'd deserve it."

"Sounds good Sam, but first we have to find the thief, or find the jewels, or preferably both. And just hope the jewels haven't been moved on."

"Agreed. So, what do you need from me now?

"Well. You showed me copy of the autopsy on Sean Kennedy, but I'd like to have another look."

"No problem Frankie, but why?"

"Call it curiosity. His death coming at the

same time as the jewels went missing, I don't know."

"I'm not fond of coincidence myself Frankie. So yes, I'll get a copy sent over. Any update on Roman Plaza?"

"Yeah, I do. I went to see the manager Mike Lee yesterday. I might have mentioned, he used to be the manager here at Acadiana."

"Yeah, I think you did. Was he helpful?"

"Very. After some initial resistance I convinced him that it was better to give me the information than have some flat-footed police detective asking questions and scaring the natives."

"Careful now Frankie, I can have you thrown in jail for disrespecting a Naples Police Detective." Frankie laughed.

"Anyway, he very kindly sent me an email with the relevant information. I'll read it to you." Frankie read the contents of Mike Lee's email to Randazzo.

"So, it looks like we have two probable suspects?"

"Seems so. Otto Kellerman and Brandon Mellor being the only two not in residence at the time of the hurricane. They have to be the most likely candidates. Having said that, we have no way to know if either of them were hiding the jewels but it's somewhere to start. I'll do some research on them, see where that takes us. Be interesting to know how soon after the hurricane each of them came back. If they had had stuff hidden, they'd want to come back as soon as possible, I guess. And if the stuff was gone, try to find out who took it. It would also be interesting to know if either of them was in town when Sean Kennedy died?"

"It would I guess," said Randazzo.

"I'll ask Mike Lee if he knows but, in the meantime, would it be possible for you to find out if or when either of them flew back around that time?"

"That's a tall order Frankie. Might take me a while to get that sort of information. It would obviously involve flight records and such. And, are we talking about November 2019 or just after the floods in 2017? If the latter, would they have come back before their condos were fit to live in?"

"Good point. Depends on how urgent they thought they needed to get back, but on balance, I think they'd wait until their own places were habitable. It would probably have taken at least a month to get things back into shape don't you think?"

"Okay, I'll try to check both sets of dates, but don't hold your breath. That's a hell of a lot of research to do. Not sure I could get that done without someone noticing. Anyway, I'll try and see what turns up. So, dates from two weeks after Irma destroyed their condos. That would be from the end of September to say end of October. And then November 2019. You check with that Mike Lee guy, okay? See if he has any records or recollection. Anything else?"

"Well, if you could do it without raising any suspicions. Any chance you could see if the original theft of the jewelry is still technically in play? I know it's a hell of a long time ago, so probably not. But they are the Crown Jewels after all. Be interesting to know. Might just be ancient history? Would it be possible to make an informal enquiry with the Irish police, the Garda I think they're called?"

"Hmm, that might be a bit tricky. I'll think on it. The last thing we need is the Irish police authorities getting any scent of this. They couldn't resist being involved in the recovery of the Irish Crown Jewels, could they, even if they think of it, as you described it, ancient history?"

"I'd guess not. Did I ever tell you my grandfather was Irish?"

"Armstrong, that's not an Irish name surely?"

"No, it was on my mother's side. The Connors of county Mayo. Crazy bunch by all accounts."

"Yeah, I can believe that" replied Sam.

"Yeah, right," said Frankie, "but hang on, since when was Sam an Italian name?" There was silence at the other end. "Sam, you still there?"

"Still here. Hmm, okay well see, my real

name isn't Sam."

"So, what is it?" asked Frankie. He heard Randazzo sigh.

"Some other time maybe, okay?"

"No, come on Sam, you can't leave it there."

"Okay. Well, it's... Stein."

"Stein!" said Frankie, why on earth Stein?"

"It's complicated. Jeez, I really regret asking about your name now. See, my dad, he was Italian, well Sicilian to be more accurate. But my mom, she was Dutch. She was a great mom, but sometimes quite stubborn. My dad wanted me to be called Salvatore, after his dad. Salvatore is Italian for Sam or Samuel. My mom, however, ... You sure you want to know all this?"

"I do," replied Frankie smiling to himself at Randazzo's obvious discomfiture.

"Well, my mom's family had a tradition of calling the first-born male child Stein. Just as her father had been called, and his father.... You get the picture? So, Stein it was, or is should I say is. Now Stein isn't exactly easy for Americans. You know every time you tell 'em, they laugh and ask why, and I have to have this same conversation over and over. So, I decided I'd call myself Sam. Simple really. But my proper name is Stein Randazzo. Happy now?"

"Fascinating," Frankie replied. "Do they know down at the station?"

"They do, cos I have to use it when I sign formal documents and all that stuff, but the novelty's worn off now, so no one mentions it anymore. Just one extra thing Frankie."

"What's that?" said Frankie.

"If you tell anyone else, I'll shoot you, okay?"

Frankie put on a mock sincere voice

"I promise," he said, unsuccessfully stifling a laugh. Randazzo cut the line

**

When he'd finished speaking to Randazzo, Charlie came and stood at Frankie's feet looking up in expectation.

"Hmm," Frankie said out loud. "I know that look. Time for a walk, is that what you're trying to tell me?" At the word walk, Charlie began to wag his tail vigorously and jumped up at Frankie's legs, then did a twirl. Frankie laughed. "Okay, you win buster, let's go."

When Frankie got back from his walk, he grabbed a coffee and sat down at his PC and read the emails and reports Barnsie had sent the previous evening. The time lag between the UK and the USA presented some coordination issues, but they'd found a satisfactory way to work around any problems it presented. Having replied with his views and conclusions on the matters presented to him by his business partner, he got up to make another coffee before sitting back down to begin some research on the two 'persons of interest' as he called them in his own mind.

He went to his PC and googled Brandon Mellor UK. He found three persons with that combination of those first and last names, but then went on to LinkedIn and found a full profile of Brandon Mellor Investment Analyst. *This has to be him*. There were details of his business and a brief bland personal profile. There was a picture, and he could see that Brandon Mellor was quite a handsome guy or he employed a very skilled photographer. Further research revealed a recent newspaper article on Mellor.

London Evening Standard
December 2019
Wealthy Investment Analysist's wife found murdered.

The brutal killing of wealthy Investment Analyst's wife, Fiona Mellor at her home in Virginia Water Surry, has shocked the local community.

Mrs. Mellor was found by her husband when he returned from a shopping trip to Maloney Bludgens the local supermarket.

Neighbors say that Mrs. Mellor was an active and popular member of the Virginia Water Community Association and sat on the board of a number of local charities. Her close friend and neighbor, Rachel Worthington said 'We're all still in shock. No one can believe Fiona is dead.

Murdered in her own home. It's quite appalling. Her poor husband Brandon is inconsolable. They were such a loving and close couple. They have no children, so Brandon is all alone now. It's a pity they abolished the death penalty" she added.

Frankie leaned back on his chair not knowing what to make of this tragic event. *Poor guy.* Then he remembered that Mike Lee had mentioned it. He couldn't see how it could possibly have any relevance to the stuff he was working on, *but you never know...?* He made some notes then, getting up from his chair, he stretched, walked out on to his lanai and took a long look at the bay. Brooding dark clouds were gathering over the Gulf, heralding some incoming bad weather.

Storms in Florida were mostly quite dramatic events, if short lived and Frankie enjoyed them, even being in the middle of them sometimes. Charlie not so much. He went to get a glass of water then came back, sat down and began to look for information on the second absentee condo owner Otto Kellerman.

Again, there were a number of people with the same name, but he found the right Otto Kellerman easily enough. Kellerman was described as a well-respected art dealer, specializing in contemporary American artists such as Ed Ruscha, Paul McCarthy, Bruce Nauman, and Mike Kelley; as well as German artists including Gerhard Richter, Sigmar Polke, and Martin Kippenberger.

We're in the right sort of general area I guess, thought Frankie.

Many of the further searches required Frankie to use Google's translation service. With some considerable patience and determination, Frankie eventually found Otto's address in Germany and his business contact details, phone number and email address. Otto and his wife Hildegard lived in Schwabing-West, described as a wealthy suburb located in the North-Western part of Munich. It was described as an affluent, residential neighborhood, with nice restaurants, bars, and cafes parks etc.

He googled Otto Kellerman Germany together with any number of variations on jewelry descriptions, antique jewelry, priceless jewelry, Irish jewelry. Antiques in general etc., but no links came up. Frankie then looked on Wikipedia and found some interesting personal history on Otto Kellerman's family. There was no mention of children, so maybe Otto was childless. Looking further Frankie discovered that Otto's father had been one of Hitler's High Command.

*

He picked up his cell and tried Otto's USA telephone number. A voice asked him to leave a message. He killed the connection without leaving a message. He would have to wait for Mike Lee to let him know when Kellerman was back at Roman Plaza before taking his enquiries any further. In the meantime, Frankie concentrated on other matters. It was the year end for his company A&B Security, so he had more than enough to do today. Frankie hated accounts and all the boring stuff to do with managing a company, but it was necessary, so he buckled down and got on with it.

There was also the matter of acknowledging the letter sent to him by the solicitor handling his divorce from Penny. She wasn't playing fair, but he was willing to let a few things slide to get the whole thing over with. *Crying shame really. I did love Penny and I'm sure she loved me, so what went wrong? Okay, so it wasn't the intense feeling I had for Hana, but that was in wartime, maybe as Hana said, feelings become intensified in such situations? Well, I'll never know will I, so no point in dwelling on it.*

*

Frankie knew from Mike Lee, that Otto Kellerman was either back at his condo, or possibly on a cruise, but that Brandon Mellor was almost certainly at his condo at Roman Plaza at the moment. He decided to go and pay a surprise visit on Mellor. Leaving his condo, Frankie walked through the car park and down Harbour Driver and into the Roman Plaza complex. He found number five and was about to press the doorbell when a voice behind him said.

"Can I help you?" Frankie turned towards the voice and saw a man striding towards him from the direction of the swimming pool. Frankie recognized Brandon from his picture on the web. In real life Brandon was tall, just over 6 ft Frankie guessed, blessed with chiseled features, a strong looking athletic body and moved with grace.

Time to take the bull by the horns.

"Oh, Hi, Brandon Mellor, isn't it?" said Frankie, "I'm Frankie Armstrong, I live in Acadiana just up the road from here. A fellow Brit." Brandon Mellor looked mildly annoyed.

"Is there something I can help you with?" said Mellor, obviously becoming exasperated.

"Maybe. The thing is, the local cops have found something of considerable value, and they think there's a possibility it may have been stolen from here. I mean here as in Roman Plaza."

"I'm sorry, what has this got to do with me, and why are you asking, not the police and what is this item?"

"Good questions. I can explain, but it may take a while. Are you okay to discuss it out here?" Mellor looked even more annoyed, but grudgingly said,

"You'd better come in." He opened the door went in and held the door open waiting. Frankie stepped into the condo, looked around and remarked.

"I heard all about the damage the flooding caused to the ground floor condos here," said Frankie looking round, "wow, they did a really good job of remodeling. Always an upside I guess."

"I guess," said Brandon frowning, "take a seat," he said gesturing towards the sofa in the middle of the room. Frankie sat. Brandon cleared some papers off the coffee table and sat down opposite Frankie. "Paperwork, never ending. Worse since my wife died."

"Yes, I heard about that, dreadful business. My sincere condolences."

"Thank you. Now you said there was something of value that may have been stolen from Roman Plaza. So, tell me, why haven't the police come to ask me? With all due respect, why send you?"

"Well, to explain. I became friends with a Detective here in Naples because of a previous situation I was involved in last year. At Acadiana actually."

"Yes, I wasn't here at the time, but I think I read about it. Something about an alligator attack. You're the guy who jumped in the Bay and tried to save the woman? Quite something." Frankie smiled a deprecating smile. *Modest..*

"Glad you think so. It was certainly exciting. Anyway, because I live nearby, the detective, Lieutenant Detective Randazzo to give him his full title, he asked me to enquire informally rather than unnecessarily upsetting anyone, you know, having the cops around. And they're overstretched. So, he thought I might find a little time to ask the residents here, before they decide if it's necessary for them to get formally involved."

"I see, said Mellor. So, what is the item in question and when was it stolen do they think?"

"I'm not at liberty to say exactly what the item is I'm afraid. It's an item of jewelry I'm sorry but I can't say that much, other than it's very valuable, apparently." Frankie could see Brandon was having some difficulty maintaining his calm disinterested appearance.

"I see," said Brandon turning his mouth down in a 'so what' expression. "And when do the police thinks this item may have been stolen?" Brandon continued.

"Just after Hurricane Irma, when the subsequent flooding wrecked your condo, along with all the others on the ground floor of course."

"I see," said Brandon again. Frankie continued,

"And as you're only too well aware, after Hurricane Irma hit, there was serious flooding which affected Roman Villas in particular. Caused serious damage to the ground floor condos here, then the mold problem... well, you know better than most what the result of that was. Apparently, everything had to be ripped out and replaced, even the ceilings and walls." Brandon nodded but said nothing "It seems that only you and your next-door neighbors, Mr. and Mrs. Kellerman, were the only residents who were absent at that time." Brandon remained silent.

"So, what Detective Randazzo thinks, is that

that situation presented an opportunity for the thief, probably one of the workers involved in the ripping out of the condos, to steal this thing, the item in question." Frankie studied Brandon's body language.

"And you can't say precisely what this 'item' is?"

"I can't I'm afraid. All they're prepared to disclose at the moment is that it's potentially very valuable."

"All sounds a bit strange to me," said Brandon. "In any event, I'm afraid I can't help you. I never leave anything of value when I leave to go back to the UK. All the stuff that was damaged, car, furniture and was covered by insurance, so..."

Brandon stood to indicate the end of the conversation and walked towards the door. Frankie stood also, then asked.

"Are you friendly with your neighbors the Kellermans?"

"Yes, we're friendly enough..., as neighbors."

"Would you know if they had anything of value stolen?"

"No, I wouldn't particularly, no." said Brandon getting a little more exasperated and opening the door.

"I believe they're on a cruise at the moment, the Kellermans?"

"Yes, Otto Kellerman said they were going. They seem to like cruising."

"Any idea when they'll be back here in Roman Plaza?"

"Not sure, Tuesday or Wednesday I think he said."

"Thanks Mr. Mellor. I don't suppose they've caught the guy?" Brandon looked at Frankie.

"What?" he said,

"Sorry, I mean the guy who broke into your house and killed your wife. I read all about it." Brandon took a deep breath, then spoke.

"No, they haven't caught the person who committed that vile act. Not yet anyway. Look thanks for coming round to ask me about this stolen valuable item, whatever it is, but I have a deal of paperwork to catch up on, so you'll excuse me..."

"Yes, of course, "said Frankie as he made to go out of the door. He turned around.

"Have you put up a reward?"

"I'm sorry?" Replied Brandon looking annoyed. "I really don't see..." Frankie cut him off. "I mean, you're a wealthy man by all accounts and I think offering a large reward often produces results in these sorts of cases." Frankie knew he was pushing it, but he carried on, "just a thought," he continued and smiled. He could see that Brandon was getting really pissed with this nosy fellow Brit.

"As it happened, I did suggest it, but the police said it wouldn't be helpful, said it would only generate a load of crazy people saying they had information. Now look I really have to go. Nice meeting you." he said, and all but pushed Frankie the rest of the way out of the door. *Boy can I be subtle when I need to be*, thought Frankie as he walked back towards Acadiana.

Once inside his own condo he made a coffee and went to sit at his PC to make some notes on the conversation before he forgot any of the details. Satisfied he had recorded the pertinent parts, he looked at his watch to check the time back in the UK, picked up his UK mobile and tapped a number in favorites. Barnsie answered on the third ring.

"Frankie boy, how's it going out there in the sunshine state? Don't ask how the weather is here, 'cos if you do, I'll put the phone down on you."

"Well good morning to you too Barnsie."

"Good afternoon, Frankie. To what do we owe the pleasure of a phone call today? Not happy with way your poor old partner is slaving away, running the business while you're out in Florida sunbathing, swimming, fishing chasing women etc. etc.?"

"Well, I think I do need to keep tabs on you, make sure you're not running off with that gorgeous secretary of yours and taking all the money."

"Cheeky bastard. Chance'd be a fine thing. Come on Frankie. Tell all. I know you wouldn't make an unscheduled call without a reason."

"You know me so well Barnsie. Thing is, my pal the detective Randazzo, you remember him?"

"Yeah, I remember, the guy you saved then nearly got killed in the process. Don't tell me he's roped you in to something else now?"

"Well, he has asked me to help him with something."

"Uh oh, I knew it, you just can't keep out of trouble when I'm not there to look after you. Come on, what is it this time?" Frankie explained everything, then said.

"Do we still use that ex CID guy Larry?"

"Of course, he's still on a retainer. Can't lose him, he's invaluable at times. Oh, I get it, let me guess, you're wanting me to get Larry to look into this guy you've just been to see, right? This Brandon Mellor. May I ask why?"

"Well by virtue of circumstance, he has to be worth looking into about the missing jewelry. And something was off. A bit hinky. I don't know."

"Okay, that instinct of yours again. What do you need?"

"Well, one of the things I'd like to find out is, if he offered to put up a reward to catch the burglar who broke in and then killed his wife. He says he offered to, but the cops said no. I find that hard to believe. We both know rewards work in instances like that. Amateur villains always have flaky friends who would sell their granny for two pence, let alone a decent amount of money."

"Okay, I can get him on to that. You want to email me all the details you have on the man, including a link to that newspaper article about his wife's death?"

"I'll do that as soon as we finish this call. But could you also ask Larry if he has any police contacts in Germany? Or any way he might be able to talk to the German authorities? I know it's a stretch but ask him anyway."

"Okay, do I need to know why?"

"No, not at this stage, just getting ahead of myself a bit, but it would be nice to know if we have that possibility."

"Okay, and I hate to ask, but how are we funding this? Okay Larry's on a retainer so it's just expenses, but even so."

"Yeah, I know, and I'll ask the detective if there's any way he can get some funding for this. It might be a case of us going official and taking this on as a formal enquiry and billing the Naples police department from A&B security."

"Sounds reasonable. In the meantime, I'll get Larry on to it as soon as you send me the details, okay? And stay out of trouble. I know you Frankie."

"I promise not to take any risks Barnsie. I learnt my lesson last time. Can't keep pushing my luck."

"Yeah, I believe you Frankie," Barnsie snorted, "thousands wouldn't. Send that stuff over." They ended the call and Frankie sent over the details then felt the need to stretch his legs and get some fresh air. "Come on Charlie, let's go for a nice long walk." They walked out of Acadiana, up Harbour Drive and left on to Crayton Road. Frankie always liked to look at the beautifully designed homes along Crayton. Fine examples of wonderful and varied architecture. All the houses had manicured lawns, with tall palm trees, leaves swaying in the breeze, shrubs planted around sumptuous flower beds. Each magnificent dwelling was styled individually. Some in the clapboard Florida Keys style, Frankie's favorite. They were typically pale blue and white with a stoop, a cabana over the two or three car garage and around the back, the inevitable luxurious swimming pool. All the gardens were a breathtaking a feast of color and variety.

Other houses were styled in pseudo grand colonial antebellum style, others Italianate in design. Even the more modern flat roof style houses, which Frankie did not approve of, still looked elegant, sitting comfortably alongside the other opulent residences. The ones on the left side of Crayton overlooked Venetian Bay at the rear and would each have a boat dock or boat lift, with an appropriate luxury boat tethered to it. Frankie smiled.

"Do you think these people realize they live in paradise Charlie?" he said as they walked along. Charlie looked up but didn't comment. They reached the end of Crayton and turned left on to Park Shore Drive, then over the bridge and down past the pretty Venetian Village which straddled both sides of Park Shore Drive, then left again and on the Park Shore proper and made for home.

*

Back at his condo at Roman Plaza, Brandon was pouring himself a large scotch, cursing himself for his stupidity in claiming he tried to put up a reward. *Why on earth did I say that? The guy could easily find out I did precisely the opposite, and that Detective Mitchell, he's already suspicious of me, I can tell. I really don't need him digging into my private affairs.*

CHAPTER 22

PRESENT

Tuesday 25 February 2020
Frankie Otto research

Early next morning, Frankie went for his usual jog. He liked to get out before the heat of the day set in, so it wouldn't be too hot for Charlie. Once back home, he showered, dressed and fed Charlie, grabbed a croissant and coffee then went out to Publix to stock up on essentials. Back home again he sat in front of his PC and dealt with the business stuff his partner Barnsie had emailed to him the previous night, along with a reminder that it was their financial year end and Frankie needed to do his bit. There was also an email from the lawyer handling his divorce. He flagged it to deal with later.

At five o'clock, he'd more or less finished the business stuff and the divorce correspondence He emailed the business documents, comments and some suggestions on presentation of the accounts to his business partner. Frankie looked at his watch. *Time for a swim and sunbathe while I wait for the arrival of Otto. Course it could be late tonight when he arrives, or maybe the pool grapevine had the wrong day or date. Who knows?* He went to change into his beachwear, then put a few beers in a cool bag and made his way down to the pool to relax in the evening sun. Most of the residents would have gone back to their condos to change for dinner, so the pool would normally be quiet at that time. He sat down opened a bottle and took a long gulp of cold beer.

"Ahh," he said, leaned back in his chair, closed eyes and let the evening sun recharge his batteries. He was almost asleep when he was woken by the sound of an email arriving on his cell phone. He sighed, picked the phone up off the table and looked at his emails. There was one new one from Mike Lee.

> *Frankie*
> *Otto and his wife arrived about ten minutes ago. I didn't tell you.*
> *Regards*
> *Mike*

Frankie looked at his watch. 5:30. *Hmm bit late to go round there now, but tomorrow I promised myself a morning fishing.* Frankie sighed, got up went quickly to his condo, changed to a T shirt and shorts then strolled down the road to Roman Plaza. He found unit six and pressed the doorbell. It opened and a frumpy looking woman opened it. She was big, red faced and scowled.

"Yes?" she said. *Fraulein Hildegard no doubt...*

"Erm, is Otto in?"

"No, he's gone to the pool. Can I help you?"

"No, it's okay thanks," said Frankie. She slammed the door and Frankie made his way to the pool. As he approached it, there was a loud splash as someone dived in. There was just the one man in the pool now, swimming up and down, so Frankie sat on one of the poolside chairs and waited. Otto eventually finished his swim, clambered out of the pool and sat a few yards away on one of the sun loungers, toweling himself dry. He looked over at Frankie.

"Hi, is that Otto Kellerman?" said Frankie waving his hand in a friendly manner. Otto squinted his eyes to see who was talking to him, then spoke.

"It is," he replied. Frankie walked over to where he stood up, still toweling himself dry. "Nothing like a nice cool relaxing swim after driving across Florida in this heat, even with air-con on full blast," said Otto.

"Amen to that," said Frankie and held out his hand and Otto automatically shook it. "I'm sorry, but do I know you?"

"No, we haven't met. My name's Frankie Armstrong and I live in Acadiana, a condo complex not too far from here. I hear you're an art expert are you not?"

"Yes, I am," said Otto looking at Frankie in

quizzical fashion. "Why do you ask?"

"Just curious. Somebody mentioned the other day that you own an art gallery. You here on business or pleasure?"

"Well, my visits here are usually a bit of both, business and pleasure. And yes, I do have an interest in a boutique art gallery in New York, but what is it to you? Who exactly are you and why are you asking these questions? And how did you know I was here? I've only just arrived back here in the last thirty minutes."

"Well, if I could just a have a few minutes of your time, I'll explain, but Mr. Mellor said you'd gone on a cruise and were coming back today, so I thought I'd pop over see if you were here."

"Yes, I see, well that's correct. We've only just arrived back from a cruise. And I have the rest of my unpacking to do, and Hildegard will be preparing dinner." He looked exasperated, hesitated then sighed loudly and said, "Okay, I suppose I can spare a little time, providing it isn't going to take too long."

"It won't I promise. See, I have a friend, a detective, works in the Naples police department. They, well he, has come across something that is presumed to have been stolen at round about the time of Hurricane Irma, or just after. It has considerable value. They've narrowed things down a bit, and it seems one strong possibility is that it was stolen by a man working on the refurbishment of the condos here at Roman Plaza."

"Well, that does sound intriguing, but what has that got to do with me? I wasn't even here then."

"That's the point really. All the condos that were damaged, well wrecked really, were on the ground floor. And apart from you and Brandon Mellor, all the other ground floor residents were here at the time Only you and Mellor were absent."

"No, sorry, I'm still not following this."

"It's obvious surely? None of the other residents would have left anything valuable in their condos while they were being ripped apart and the internal structures rebuilt. They would have taken any such valuables with them, or at least stored them in a separate safe place. The only people who couldn't do that, if they had to, were you and Brandon Mellor because you weren't here, were you?"

"Yes, okay, I see now," said Kellerman disingenuously. "So, what was the item in question, this thing that was allegedly stolen?"

"Jewels," said Frankie. Otto looked surprised.

"Jewels?" Otto repeated, looking perplexed.

"Yes jewelry, why?" said Frankie.

"No, nothing, please, do go on with your story."

"Well, more than that I don't know. It was really just a matter of tidying up as it were. You know, making sure that neither you nor your neighbor Brandon Mellor weren't missing anything of value. Anything that might have been taken when they were in ripping the walls out and ceilings etc., you know, during the refurbishment of your condos."

"We never leave anything of value when we're not here, so the answer is no. And if we had had something taken, we'd have reported it to the authorities on our return. And as we are well insured, we would have made a claim. But no, we're not missing anything." Otto stayed silent for a moment then said. "Well, Mr. Armstrong, isn't it? It's been very nice to meet you, but I have to go now. Sorry I couldn't help. By the way, why on earth are the police asking you to make enquiries?"

"Like I said, its nothing official, Sam, that's Sam Randazzo the detective, knowing I lived nearby, he just asked me to ask around, that's all." Otto raised his eyebrows obviously doubting the casual explanation.

"Well, have a nice evening. Goodbye," said Kellerman abruptly.

"You too Mr. Kellerman," said Frankie and sat back down in his chair again.

Frankie watched Otto make his way to his condo, he seemed deep in thought.

"Hallo Liebling," Otto shouted as he entered his apartment.

"Hallo Otto," came the distant answer, "in the bedroom just finishing unpacking. See anyone interesting at the pool, any interesting gossip to tell me? Oh, I forgot, there was a man here looking for you."

"Yes, I met him Hildi. A nosy Brit from down the road, that Acadiana place, asking if we were missing anything after the floods, you know after the hurricane?" Hildegard came out of the bedroom into the lounge.

"Oh, who was asking again?"

"Man called Frankie Armstrong. Like I said, he lives in Acadiana, English guy, said he's asking on behalf of some detective. Wanted to know if we'd had anything taken or lost anything from our apartment when Irma did all that damage."

"And did you tell him?"

"Tell him what Liebling?"

"Sorry, yes of course, sorry."

*

Otto Kellerman was born just after WW2. The war had ended in 1945 when Nazi Germany had been defeated and unconditionally surrendered in May that year. Then in August 1945, Japan also surrendered unconditionally, after the United States had dropped atomic bombs on Hiroshima and Nagasaki on the 6th and 9th of August.

As Soviet troops had entered the heart of Berlin in the previous April, Hitler had allegedly committed suicide in his underground bunker. It was claimed Hitler shot himself. Then Eva

Braun, whom Hitler had recently married, is said to have taken her own life in the same manner.

Otto's mother told him how, as the war came to an end, his father had risked his life to get back home to see his son and daughter one final time, before fleeing Germany in accordance with a pre-arranged plan. Some of the high-ranking German officers had surrendered, while others, including Otto's father, General Heinric Kellerman, had chosen to cut and run and start a new life elsewhere.

Heinric Kellerman had left instructions with his wife, including one that said his son Otto, must be enrolled at The Academy of Fine Arts in Munich (Akademie der Bildenden Künste München). Located in the Maxvorstadt district of Munich, the academy was one of the oldest and most significant art academies in Germany. And so it was, in accordance with his father's wishes, that Otto became a scholar there. He had little idea why his father had insisted on him taking this course, but he had some natural talent as an artist, so thoroughly enjoyed the subject and even excelled at it.

While at the Akademie der Bildenden Künste, Otto met his future wife Hildegard Neumann, a promising artist in her own right. Hildegard's father had served the German war machine as a U boat commander. Otto Neumann was amongst the most successful submarine commanders and completed 16 patrols, sinking forty-six enemy ships and damaging a further four. His luck ran out in 1942 when his submarine was torpedoed and sunk by an America destroyer in what was known as the battle of the Atlantic. Neumann died with the rest of his crew.

Otto was not typically Germanic in appearance, being only 5 ft 6" with dark hair and brown eyes, but nevertheless possessed a certain charm and had little trouble attracting girlfriends. Otto also found his talent as an artist useful for persuading his girlfriends to disrobe early in their relationship so he could paint them. Hildegard was different. She and Otto fell in love at first sight.

On his 21st Birthday his mother presented Otto with a bulky envelope containing a long letter and other documents. She told him his father had left it with her when he'd come home briefly after the war, along with the instructions regarding his education. Otto took the package to his bedroom. He sat on his bed and read the letter over and over again. Tears sprang to his eyes and ran liberally down his cheeks as he read some of the things his father had written to his 'Dearly beloved son'.

It was a pivotal moment in Otto's life and things were about to become much clearer to him. His father had said in the letter, that he considered his primary duty was to his own family and in particular his only son Otto. *War was necessary*, he said, *to take what is ours by right, to conquer and to dominate. We may have lost this time, but we Nazis will be back, stronger than ever. It will not be long before the Fourth Reich emerges and with even greater strength and irresistible power. We will succeed in the end. It is our God given right.*

And yes, he had taken valuable items from the enemy, but as far as he was concerned, they were the spoils of war and as such, belonged to him. He in turn was bequeathing them to Otto.

He said that if he, Otto, disagreed with this philosophy, then he was free to turn the items over to the authorities. But that it was his sincere desire for Otto to possess these rare works of art, enjoy and use them to enhance his life in any way he wished. His father went on to say. You will learn in life young Otto, that not all people and races are equal. *You and I Otto, we're descended from the Proto-Aryans, a superior race and original dwellers of north Germany. Indeed, it is quite possible these people in turn were descendants of the peoples of the lost continent of Atlantis. Hitler himself believed this. Do not ever forget Otto, we are Herrenmenschen. Be strong, survive and prosper, the weak deserve nothing and are to be despised.*

He put the letter to one side and examined the list of items his father had plundered. There were numerous works of art listed, most of which Otto hade some knowledge of. He could hardly believe these were now effectively his. The location of the paintings was also revealed in the documents. Otto was surprised to find they had never left Germany. He was also surprised to find he was the owner of a small house near Rothenburg ob der Tauber in Bavaria. The ownership documents were lodged with a bank in his name, together with instructions for access. The documents also revealed the precise location of the hidden paintings within the building.

Otto put the papers to one side and tried to absorb the avalanche of information that had been disclosed in the documents. He felt overwhelmed and was desperate to share news of his good fortune but knew he could never reveal any of the information to anyone. He began to think what this meant. Even at this early stage of the discovery he realized the limitations of being able to exploit this massive treasure trove. Otto was blessed with his father's high intellect and cunning and realized at once that attempting to sell any of these works of art entailed huge personal risk. And, in any event, he already felt the love of possession of these unique artifacts.

He would put his mind to the task of how to make the most of his father's gift. Already the faintest glimmer of an idea began to form in his mind, but he would take his time, no rush. First, he needed to plan a visit to his house in Bavaria where he could feast his eyes on his new possessions. He felt an almost sexual thrill of anticipation.

CHAPTER 23

PRESENT

Wednesday 26 February 2020
Frankie and Randazzo

The next day, Frankie awarded himself the morning off. He went down to Naples Bay Resort and hired a small center console fishing boat and set off down the Gordon River estuary, past the riverside mansions and out into the Gulf of Mexico. It was another glorious Florida day and there were plenty of other fishermen out in the Gulf. He caught snapper, pompano and a hammerhead shark which took some landing. Then he hit a run of Spanish mackerel and had a ball.

He'd lost all sense of time but then was suddenly feeling extremely hungry and realized it was past lunchtime. He was also tired, hot, and thirsty, but nevertheless felt elated and relaxed. Back in his condo, he showered, had a bite to eat then called Barnsie his business partner in the UK.

"You're calling for an update I guess?" said

Barnsie, never one to waste time on idle chatter.

"I am."

"Okay, well, Larry contacted the detective handling the Mellor murder and got some interesting info. Look, why don't I get Larry to call you direct. Less chance of wires getting crossed."

"Good idea. In the meantime, if our IT genius Gareth has any spare time, can you ask him to see what he can find on Brandon Mellor and also on a guy called Otto Kellerman, an art dealer who lives in Germany, in Schwabing-West, a suburb of Munich?" Frankie spelt out Otto's name and the name of the suburb. "Not the usual stuff on Wikipedia, I can find all that myself. And tell Gareth I'll sort him out for his time when I get back."

"Will do. Better go, got another call waiting. Be safe Frankie." Frankie was in the middle of making a coffee when Larry called. After going through the greetings, Larry got to it.

"Okay, so this Mellor guy. I talked to the detective. Guy called Robert Mitchell who's handling the case. He likes to be called Mitch. Anyway, Mitch was very forthcoming. He was curious as to why we were asking, so a bit hesitant at first, but I told him you were working with the Naples police department just checking out a few things. He knows that Mellor has a condo in Naples, so he relaxed a bit. I get the impression he doesn't particularly like Mellor's story about the break in, when his wife got killed. All a bit too pat he says."

"When I repeated what Mellor had told you about the reward suggestion, he laughed. that's exactly arse about face says he. I suggested he put up a reward and Mellor declined. Made some excuse about it being disrespectful to his late wife's memory or some such bullshit. Said that if the police did their work properly, they wouldn't need him to put up a reward. You can imagine how well that went down?"

"Interesting," said Frankie. "Anything else?"

"Only that Mellor's' bullshit response to your question re the reward has reinforced his view that Mellor is lying about the whole thing. Thinks Mellor might have killed his wife. He's looking for a motive but can't find one so far, maybe insurance he thinks. No affairs reported or suspected, no friends saying they were unhappy. Model husband apparently."

"Okay, thanks for that. I'll think on it. How about Germany? I've given Barnsie the details of a guy called Otto." Larry interjected.

"Yeah, he sent them over already. I don't have any direct contact, but as they say, I do know a man who possibly does. Guy called Eric Noble. He was in Interpol. Took early retirement. Got injured in some raid on a terrorist cell in Germany, so my guess is he'll still have some contacts. I can give it a whirl anyway. We both joined the police on the same day, and we still talk occasionally. I'll let you know how it goes."

"Thanks Larry," said Frankie and finished

the call. Charlie was sitting looking up at him. "Yes, okay Charlie. You play me like a fiddle, don't you?" and he went to get Charlie's leash. On his return to his condo, Frankie was about to email Randazzo with an update when he remembered that this was all unofficial at the moment and it might not be wise to leave a paper trail. He picked up his cell.

"Frankie. News?" said Randazzo as soon as he answered.

"Just an update. Nothing startling yet, but some interesting bits and pieces. He told the detective about his chats with Brandon Mellor and Otto Kellerman.

"Both conversations were inconclusive, but at least I've now made contact. So, it's more research and then I'll have another crack at them." Frankie then told Randazzo about his subsequent conversation with Larry.

"So, he's ex CID. Useful guy to have on your payroll. And he says the detective looking into Mrs. Mellor's murder has the husband Brandon down for the killing?"

"That's what he said. And the fact that Brandon lied about putting up a reward has only served to increase his suspicions."

"Interesting, said Randazzo, "you could think that maybe Mellor doesn't want the killer found? But why?"

"Maybe Brandon employed someone to kill his wife for the insurance money? Wouldn't be the first time someone has paid to have their spouse knocked off for the insurance payout."

"That's true," said the detective, "but either way, it doesn't help us regarding the jewels. And what did you make of this Otto character?"

"Difficult to say. I need to do more digging and thinking. My initial research revealed that he's quite wealthy, lives in a nice house near Munich. Well respected art dealer by all accounts."

"Does art include stolen artifacts, as in antique jewelry do you think?"

"No, he's quite specialized. Paintings exclusively it seems, and his particular specialty is claimed to be contemporary American art."

"Hmm, so unlikely to be interested in stolen jewelry, or any obvious connection to Ireland," said Randazzo.

"Unlikely but not impossible. Let's keep an open mind. There is an interesting fact about him though. His father was a high ranking general in the Nazi movement. One of Hitler's High Command for a while. That is until Hitler started losing it and sacked him."

"Well, I guess it's interesting in a way, but not really useful to us, is it?"

"Nope, I guess not. And as you say, no obvious link to Ireland or any involvement in stolen jewelry."

"Ah well, keep turning stones over, something will turn up, you never know.

And thanks for the information to date. Keep me in the loop."

"Will do, but before you go Sam, there is something. As I said, I was happy to give my services free for the initial part of the investigation, but that was on the basis that you'd be taking it inhouse pretty soon, as it were. I understand your reluctance to do that, now there's a possible international aspect to it, but apart from my time, we have to pay Larry and so on."

"Yeah, I've been thinking about that and I'm going to talk to my boss eventually, explain the whole thing. He's quite a discreet guy. I'm going to recommend we find a way to fund you so that you can keep on it, providing you want to of course?"

"I do Sam, I'd like to see this through right to the end if possible."

"Okay, leave it with me. I won't let you down. And let me know any further developments." They bid each other goodbye.

CHAPTER 24

PRESENT

Friday 28 February 2020
Larry's update

It was Friday lunchtime before Larry called back.

"Do you want the interesting news or the more interesting news?"

"I'll take the interesting news first Larry," Frankie replied laughing.

"They've issued a warrant for the arrest of Brandon Mellor in connection with the death of Fiona Mellor. Not sure what the protocols are for extraditing him from Florida, but it's now in play."

"Wow, they have some new evidence presumably?"

"Not sure, they wouldn't say. And though it's, theoretically at least, in the public arena, maybe you should keep quiet about it for the time being?"

"Okay, right. Now that is interesting, but you say you have even more interesting news. Come on, I'm intrigued."

"Spoke to my pal Eric Noble, the one I told you about."

"Yes, I remember," said Frankie.

"So, he called his old contact over there in Germany and asked about Otto Kellerman, the art collector from Munich. His pal said to wait, and he'd check if there was anything on the system about him. The guy came back to the phone and said another guy would call him back. Eric reckons our enquiry must have tripped a switch on their system. So, about an hour later this other guy calls Eric back, guy called Karl Becker. He wants to know everything about what, why and who etc."

"So, Eric calls me back and tells me to expect a call from Becker. He called me and I told him what I knew, which wasn't that much. I told him I was really just making and enquiry on your behalf and that you were working on something with the police in Naples Florida that may or may not involve this Otto character. I hope you don't mind, but I gave him your cell number and he's going to call you direct?"

"No, I don't mind at all Larry. Sounds like this could get interesting. Thanks, I'll await Mr. Becker's call."

"Great," said Larry, "and if you don't mind, would you keep me in the loop. It's like being back at the CID when we got into a good one. Got to admit, I still miss the excitement of the chase."

"I'll keep you in the loop Larry, but at the moment I don't have anything other than the vaguest idea that Kellerman might have been up to no good. Still, like you say, must be something to get the German authorities so interested in knowing why we enquired." Frankie ended the call and thought about what he'd just been told by Larry. Then he looked online for information about extradition between the USA and UK. There was a bilateral agreement signed in 2003, but the further Frankie looked into it, the more confused he became. He called Detective Randazzo.

"You calling about this Brandon guy and the arrest warrant just been issued in the UK?"

"Yes Sam. That didn't take long."

"No, it didn't. The British cops know his address here in Naples, so they know it's in our jurisdiction. I saw the message come in. they've contacted us on an informal basis at the moment."

"How do you mean, informal?"

"Well, they'll probably file for extradition, but that's a long and tedious and not always a successful process. So, they're asking for our cooperation. Guy called here and spoke to my Chief, asked if we would go talk to Brandon Mellor, ask him if he'd be willing to return voluntarily."

"And will the department send someone to talk to him? I mean, what advantage is there for Mellor by returning voluntarily?" Asked Frankie.

"Couple of reasons he might want to. It's only an arrest warrant and if he's innocent, he should be confident enough to go back and straighten things out. Prove he's not the perp. If he doesn't, he'll look guilty as hell, and they'll get him back eventually."

"Yes, I can see why that might work,"

"And," continued Randazzo, "they'll freeze his assets. Leastways they'll apply to freeze his assets. He's got his house up for sale, but they'll also try to freeze his bank accounts. Either way, if he is innocent, he'd be smart to go back as soon as possible."

"Are you going to see him?"

"No, not me. I dodged the issue. Said I was too busy on other stuff. Suggested the department ask someone else to go and talk to him. I'd prefer not to get directly involved at this stage. In any event, all the department can do at the moment is send someone to have an informal word with him. I'm sure the British authorities will have already contacted him directly. I guess they think if we go to see him, it will increase the pressure, make him aware that we're keeping an eye on him as well."

"I can see that," said Frankie.

"Then again," said Randazzo, "maybe he's hopping mad and innocent and will go back to clear his name. Clear up any misunderstanding. As it stands, we certainly don't have any solid information ourselves to take action against him,"

"Do I still pursue the possibility of him being involved somehow in the jewelry theft though?" Frankie asked.

"Yeah, one thing might be related to the other, but maybe not? Let's carry on with our plan and see where it takes us. By the way, I'm still working on how to get a meeting scheduled with the Chief to get some sort of budget for our little project. I hope you don't mind waiting a bit longer. I'm sure I can get a budget approved but I have to choose my moment."

"Okay Sam, no problem." Frankie broke the connection.

While he waited for the German police guy Becker to call back, Frankie decided to do some more research into the theft of the Irish Crown jewels, focusing particularly on the main suspect Frank Shackleton. Frank Shackleton, Frankie discovered, was the younger brother of the intrepid polar explorer Ernest Shackleton. Frankie googled some more and found an interesting article that appeared in The Irish Times in 1968 that suggested that Shackleton, working in conjunction with Captain Richard Gorges, stole Sir Arthur Vicars's keys one night after Vicars had gotten drunk. Shackleton allegedly then took the jewels, hid them somewhere to collect later and returned the keys to Vicar's possession, as if nothing had happened. As likely as it may have been, the authorities couldn't produce enough reliable evidence to prove anything, and Shackleton was never formally accused of the crime.

However, later, Frank Shackleton was jailed after being convicted of banking fraud in 1913. It's claimed, he changed his name when he was released several years later then disappeared without a trace.

Frankie was intrigued. He googled some more and came across a letter written to a magazine called History of Ireland. He read the letter. It contained much more detail on Frank Shackleton than he'd come across before.

FRANK SHACKLETON

Published in 20th-century / Contemporary History, Issue 1 (Spring 2002), Letters, Volume 10

Sir, I read with interest Tomás O'Riordan's article on the theft of the Irish Crown Jewels. I have written an entry on Francis Richard ('Frank') Shackleton for the Royal Irish Academy's Dictionary of Irish Biography and thought that your readers might be interested in some further information regarding his later life. After the theft of the jewels and the subsequent investigation, he was involved in some dubious business deals, being declared bankrupt in1910 with debts of nearly £85,000. He fled to Portuguese West Africa where he initially worked as a plantation manager but was arrested in October 1912 on fraud charges and sent back to London for trial. Charged with the 'fraudulent conversion' of funds entrusted to him by a Miss Mary Browne, he was found guilty at his trial at the Old Bailey in October 1913 and sentenced to fifteen months hard labour. On his release from prison his brother, the Antarctic explorer Sir Ernest Shackleton, secured him a position in a London office. Little is known of what he did for the next few years. He was living at Sydenham in 1920 but by 1934 he had moved to Chichester where he opened an antique shop and also worked as a genealogist. He lived there with his unmarried sister, Amy Vibert Shackleton for the rest of his life and died at St Richard's Hospital on 24 June 1941. Buried in Chichester cemetery...
DAVID KENNEDY

Royal Irish Academy
Dictionary of Irish Biography
Dublin

Using the information he'd found in the letter to the History of Ireland magazine, Frankie undertook some further research and came across something that stopped him in his tracks, *Well I'll be dammed! Is this the proverbial smoking gun?* Frankie's cell signaled an incoming call. He looked, an international number....

"Hello Frankie Armstrong." Becker had the slightest hint of an accent but otherwise spoke flawless English.

"Hello, Mr. Armstrong, my name is Detective Karl Becker. I work in the BKA, the Federal Criminal Police Department in Germany I think you may be expecting my call, yes?"

"I am yes. How can I help Mr. Becker?"

"We're curious why you're making enquiries about Otto Kellerman. What is the American angle may I ask?"

"At the moment, it's an informal investigation into a missing artifact. Detective Sam Randazzo of the Naples Police department asked me to look into matters on his behalf. It's a long story, but the condo complex I live in in Naples, is also near to Roman Plaza where Otto Kellerman and his wife have a condo, an apartment."

"Yes, we are aware of the condo in question. Is Herr Kellerman suspected of involvement in the theft of this artifact? And if so, how valuable is this item?"

"Last question first. The item is potentially worth a huge amount of money. I don't think I'm at liberty to tell you precisely what it is, but I can tell you it is an item of jewelry. And there's no evidence currently that would suggest Mr. Kellerman's involvement in the theft." Frankie went on to explain the situation regarding Sean Kennedy and Mrs. Kennedy. Karl Becker remained silent and didn't interrupt. When Frankie had finished, Becker spoke.

"Okay, I understand. I will text you my contact details and perhaps you will let me know if there are any developments that involve Herr Kellerman. Is there any information you would like from me?"

"The obvious question," said Frankie. Why did you react in the way you did to our enquiry about Kellerman?"

"Are you a police officer Mr. Armstrong?"

"No, I am a partner in a security company in the UK. I happen to live in Naples as a long-term condo renter. Detective Randazzo and I have collaborated on a previous investigation, so he asked for my help in investigating this matter. I understand if you feel you can't tell me about a confidential police matter, so maybe it would be better if you spoke directly to Detective Randazzo." There was silence on the line. "Hello" said Frankie thinking maybe the connection had been lost.

"Yes, I'm still here," said Becker, "I think in the circumstances I can tell you why we're looking at the activities of Herr Kellerman. I assume you have done some research into Kellerman and know that he's an art dealer?"

"Yes, I do," said Frankie.

"Did you also know his father was a high-ranking officer in Hitler's High Command?"

"Yes, I found that out by doing some basic enquiries on the internet."

"Okay, well we suspect that during the Third Reich, Kellerman's father, along with certain other individuals we've identified, were heavily involved in the organized looting of property, right up until the end of the war. We strongly suspect that General Heinric Kellerman, was a leading figure in organizing military units known as the Kunstschutz, who stole huge amounts of gold, silver, currency, cultural items including paintings, ceramics, books and religious treasures etc."

"Some of these stolen items were recovered, but many remain hidden, and we believe are now in the possession of the families of those whose parents organized and participated in the plundering."

"So, you believe his son Otto is somehow involved?"

"We and other organizations have an on-going interest in all aspects of this missing trove of plundered treasures. Many of the people who were involved in the original thefts have now passed away, so it is their families who survived them which are the main focus of our attention these days."

"And do you have any actual evidence that Kellerman junior is involved in the way you think, or is it merely supposition?" Frankie asked.

"Put it this way. We have more than suspicions but no hard evidence to make any charges or moves against various people, including Herr Kellerman."

"You think Otto Kellerman is somehow selling these stolen treasures?"

"We think his business activities, being an art dealer, provide a useful cover for dealing in stolen art, yes. And we do have one thread as it were, which may unravel to reveal something, I don't know, but I'm going to share this with you in the event you observe some activity over there that may help. Maybe Kellerman will not be so careful away from the prying eyes of the German authorities, yes?"

"I see where you're going. So what information is it you wish to share."

"A couple of months ago, there was a complaint from a minor, a young girl who said she'd been photographed in an inappropriate way. Said that the man had picked her up in a street café and told her she was model material. I know, but young girls still fall for that sort of stuff. Anyway, her complaint was taken seriously and resulted in a raid on the photographer's premises and home, a man called Günter Müller."

"At Muller's premises, they found pictures of young girls, but nothing really pornographic. Borderline, but not bad enough to charge him. However, what was found at his home was a large amount of cash which he couldn't account for. Further investigation of the individual followed, and it transpired from his financial records, that one of his clients for his photography services is Otto Kellerman."

"We were alerted. There's a flag on the police database, the same one which was also tripped when your colleague made his enquiry. We had hoped we might find pictures of stolen art, but no, nothing. But the man, the photographer, Hans Feigler, remains under suspicion and his cash was confiscated pending further developments. The peculiar thing is, we couldn't find any pictures of Kellerman's legitimate pieces of art on his computers either. The man was questioned and simply clammed up when asked to explain the absence of such pictures."

"So, what do you think Otto Kellerman is doing?"

"We suspect there's an American connection. We know of course that he is a part owner of an art gallery in New York and that somehow, he's using that place to sell the stolen art in America, but it's a suspicion at the moment and no more."

"And do you think it would be possible for him to ship any of the stolen art out of Germany to America?"

"Not impossible, but unlikely. And it's not just Germany, but Switzerland. Much of the plundered artifacts from World War Two are said to be hidden in the deep vaults of the Swiss banks. He might have got away with exporting the odd piece of artwork, the odd picture, but we've had him and others, under observation for many years, so doubtful."

"Okay. Does he travel abroad a lot?"

"Not really. Apart from some business trips to China, he and his wife only ever travel to America."

"And why does he travel to China, do you know?"

"He buys frames from China. Apparently, the Chinese produce the quality of picture frames he likes for the legitimate paintings he sells. The frames are part of the overall attraction of this particular genre of art, he claims on his website."

"And does that claim hold up?"

"We asked an independent expert and he confirmed that the wood and the techniques the

Chinese use produce a unique quality of picture frame, and that they are highly prized in the art world., So yes, these visits seem to be legitimate business trips."

"So where does that leave Otto Kellerman?" Asked Frankie.

"Until our suspicions are confirmed one way or another, Otto Kellerman remains a well-respected member of German society and a man of integrity."

"Okay Mr. Becker, where do we go from here?"

"Karl, please call me Karl. I will send you my contact details and let's keep in touch. I will let you know any developments that may be pertinent to you and please do likewise for me, agreed?"

"Agreed," said Frankie and gave Becker his email address.

CHAPTER 25

PRESENT

Friday 28 February 2020
Frankie and Daisy Cibao

It was Friday evening and Frankie, and Daisy were sitting at their usual table in Cibao. Frankie was sporting a new yellow linen shirt, Daisy looked stunning in a red dress, *when doesn't she?* thought Frankie. Daisy was a 5 ft 7", shortish blonde hair, green-brown eyes, a captivating smile and she was smart. She was also no slouch when it came to self-defense as Frankie knew to his cost when she'd challenged him to a fight.

"Come on, attack me, like you mean it," she'd said one day in his condo when they were talking about how vulnerable women were. He took the challenge thinking it was just a bit of fun, but she put him on the floor in a matter of seconds. He had another go and this time without holding back. It took him all his time to overwhelm her, but this was with foreknowledge and

Frankie could handle himself, so he concluded the average man, innocent of her capabilities, would be no match for Daisy.

Tonight, she was wearing a tight red number which didn't leave too much to the imagination. They sat down and a man found her so interesting, he was looking backwards after he'd passed their table and ploughed straight into a waiter serving drinks on a table further down. They had to stifle a laugh. Frankie said,

"You do it on purpose don't you? That dress I mean. You're without shame Daisy Metcalf." She smiled a wicked smile.

"Only occasionally. You want me to take it off Frankie?" she said smiling coquettishly.

"I do, said Frankie, "but not here and not now. That poor man would have a heart seizure, along with a few other diners I reckon. Now be a good girl and tell me what you'd like to drink." They ordered drinks then their starters and main courses. Frankie had the special, Wall-Eyed Pike, Daisy had the pork chop. They chatted about Daisy's latest assignment, then the conversation turned to what progress Frankie had made with the investigation. He then told her about researching Brandon Mellor's family history.

"And?" asked Daisy, "anything to connect him directly with the stolen Irish Crown Jewels or whatever they were?"

"I'd rather not say at the moment. I think I can. So, I plan to go and see him in the very near future. After that I'll tell you all."

"Ooh, I like a man of mystery," said Daisy in a humorous mocking voice. "What about this Otto character?" she asked. "Anything you can tell me about him?"

"Yes, I can, but again, a lot of supposition and not much hard evidence."

"I'm happy with the supposition. After all, facts don't really matter to me, I'm a reporter don't forget. Suppositions and scandalous gossip are food and drink to the likes of me." She raised her glass to toast Frankie. He laughed. "So come on tell all." Daisy remained quiet while Frankie related the various conversations and what he'd discovered, then what he'd been told by the German policeman. Frankie stopped and took a long glug of his wine.

"Amazing," said Daisy. "People who live in Naples all seem so, I don't know, ordinary, respectable, then you dig a little bit and..." she left the sentence unfinished and took a sip of wine.

"Yes, but in this case, though there's lots of suspicion, and interesting though all that may be, like I said, there's not much in the way of hard facts is there? Leastwise not yet."

*

It was Saturday and Frankie had a slightly different routine to the weekdays. Normally if they'd been out on a Friday night Daisy would have stayed over, but she said she had an assignment on the Saturday, so wanted an early start to drive across to Miami. Frankie rose a bit later than normal, took Charlie out for a short walk, then took him back to the condo and went to Publix and The Food Market to stock up on food and other essentials. Daisy said she'd be back early evening, so Frankie said he'd cook dinner for her at his place.

At midday, Frankie got a call from Detective Randazzo.

"Sorry you couldn't get hold of me yesterday, Frankie, out of town on a missing persons case. Any news?" Frankie filled him in on the latest developments regarding Otto Kellerman.

"Okay, well that might put him in the frame for dealing in old and stolen artifacts in general, but the Irish angle? That doesn't make sense to me. If Kellerman is dealing in stolen art, or valuables, whatever, sounds like he's got plenty to go at if the suspicions of the German police about him are well founded. How and why would a guy like that get involved in stolen Irish jewelry?"

"I don't disagree," said Frankie, "especially in view of what I might have discovered about our friend Brandon. Do you know how the interview with Brandon Mellor went?" Asked Frankie.

"Yeah, Mellor's going back voluntarily. Probably flying back in the next couple of days. So, come on Frankie, what about Brandon Mellor, what have you discovered?"

"Might be something, but I'd rather not say for the moment."

"You're being mysterious Frankie, come on give."

"I'd rather not, not just for the minute. I want to be absolutely sure before I say anything. You understand Sam?"

"Okay, okay, I guess I'll have to wait. So, you got a next move?"

"Yes, I do. Can you find out what day Brandon is planning to travel back to the UK Sam?

"If he's told my guy, then no problem. I'll see if I can get hold of him now, call you back." Frankie sat on the lanai, looking out over the bay and weighing up his options. His cell signaled an incoming call. Randazzo.

"Hi Sam."

"He told Detective Robins, that's the guy who went to talk to Brandon. He told him he's planning to go back this Sunday. That's tomorrow. Said he was going to get in touch with the detective, Mitchell, handling his wife's murder, to tell him he's going back. Robins said he seemed good and mad about it all. Said Mellor seemed genuine, said you could almost believe he didn't do it."

"So, I'm going to have to move fast if I'm going to talk to him about my hunch."

"You are Frankie. Well good luck and be sure to let me know what happens."

"You'll be the first to know Sam."

CHAPTER 26

PRESENT

Saturday 29 February
Frankie confronts Brandon Mellor

Frankie had gone to Brandon Mellor's condo mid-morning but got no answer. He just hoped Brandon hadn't decided to go home a day early. He went back to his own condo to get on with some outstanding business matters, then a couple of hours later he walked back to Roman Plaza to see if Brandon had returned. He didn't want to call ahead and give Brandon any chance to refuse to meet him and thought it would be better if he arrived unannounced. At just before three o'clock Frankie pressed Brandon's condo doorbell. Nothing. He pressed again, no response. *Drat!* He was just about to walk away when the door opened. Brandon Mellor looked annoyed, his reading glasses hitched up on his head.

"What is it this time? I'm leaving tomorrow and I have a great deal of paperwork to complete. So, unless this is something urgent, then can we please leave it till another time, when I came back, okay?" Brandon started to shut the door. Frankie wedged his foot in it to stop it closing. "What the fuck do you think you're doing. Get your foot out of the way."

"I need to talk to you about Frank Shackleton." Brandon looked confused then seemed to gather himself together.

"I have no idea what you're talking about. I don't know any person called Shackleton."

"Oh, I think you do," said Frankie. And with a mighty push, he shoved the condo door open wide sending Brandon stumbling backwards into his condo, struggling to remain upright. He just about managed it, by which time Frankie was in the condo and had the door closed behind him. Frankie could see that Brandon was considering a charge at him. "Don't," said Frankie, nevertheless preparing to be rushed at. Brandon hesitated, then flopped down on the couch. Frankie took a chair opposite and placed his cell phone on the coffee table "That's better."

"You want to go first, or shall I?" said Frankie. Brandon turned up both hands in a gesture of *I don't' care*. "Okay, me first then," said Frankie. "You're of Irish heritage are you not?"

"I believe my ancestors were Irish, yes, so what? Lots of people in the UK have Irish heritage."

"How is your Irish history?"

"What? Look, I haven't got time to play games. As your detective friend has no doubt informed you, I'm going back to the UK tomorrow to clear up these crazy accusations about me being involved in my wife's murder. So, if you don't mind..."

"I think you know what I'm talking about all right. Your grandfather was Frank Shackleton, brother of the famous Antarctic explorer Ernest Shackleton." Brandon Mellor's mouth opened as if he was going to speak, then he closed it. Frankie waited then continued. "In October 1912 Frank Shackleton was sent to England to face trial on charges of fraud. To be precise," Frankie looked at the notes he'd taken whilst researching Frank Shackleton, "Francis Shackleton was charged with the 'fraudulent conversion' of funds entrusted to him by a Miss Mary Browne and found guilty at his trial at the Old Bailey in October 1913. He was sentenced to fifteen months hard labor." Mellor finally found his voice. He coughed a little cough, then spoke.

"Well, I'm sure this is all very interesting, but what has it got to do with me?"

"I think you know full well what it's got to do with you. On his release from prison, Frank Shackleton changed his name to Frank Mellor, then settled in the south of England. He had a son called William Mellor, who in turn had two children, Samantha Mellor and Brandon Mellor. Frank Shackleton is in fact your grandfather.

How'm I doing so far?"

"Okay, big deal, so what?" said Brandon, his voice belligerent, but his eyes betraying him.

"You know all this but I'm going to say it anyway." Brandon shrugged. "In 1907 Frank Shackleton allegedly stole the Irish Crown Jewels from Dublin Castle. He'd taken the keys from Sir Arthur Vicars who was drunk as a skunk at the time. He stole the jewels from the strongbox and then hid them before returning the keys to Sir Arthur's possession. He then played dumb about the whole thing."

"As you also know, he was accused of the theft, but no hard evidence was found, to be able to convict him. The jewels were presumably too hot to sell on at that time. That would risk him being caught, so he held on to them. Eventually he passed them on to his son William. William in turn passed them on to his son, you, Brandon Mellor." Frankie stopped talking and looked at Brandon.

"Supposition, nothing more," said Brandon. "You have absolutely nothing to back that story up, so stop wasting my time. I told you, I have things to do."

"You're right Brandon. But now we have the jewels, they'll be forensically examined," Frankie said confidently. "I don't know if the results will come back before your departure tomorrow, but I'd be surprised if the forensic people didn't eventually find some trace of your

DNA on the jewels." The color drained from Brandon's face.

"You have them, the Crown Jewels?" Brandon stuttered. Frankie nodded. "How, where...?"

"I take it from your response, that you now acknowledge, the jewels were in your condo until hurricane Irma came along?" Brandon looked at Frankie, hesitated, then nodded and hung his head in defeat. Frankie waited.

"Shit," said Brandon. He stood up walked around then sat down again then said, "shit shit shit!" and banged the coffee table so hard, Frankie's cell fell off. Frankie retrieved it and placed it back on the table.

"You want to tell me more?"

"I can't," Brandon said, all the bluster gone now. Frankie couldn't help feeling a little sorry for him. "it's complicated."

"It always is," said Frankie. "So, you're going back tomorrow to turn yourself in? Do you intend to admit to your wife's murder?" Frankie asked while he judged Brandon was inclined to talk honestly. Brandon looked up and stared Frankie in the eye, his face contorted in anger, his teary eyes fierce. He sniffed, then stared hard at Frankie before he stood up and shouted.

"I did not kill my wife. Don't you understand?" he screamed at Frankie with considerable ferocity. Frankie was taken aback. Brandon continued, spittle flying from his lips "I loved Fiona more than anything in the world. That's why they did it." Brandon sat and sobbed. There was no doubting his passion. Frankie gave him a minute, then said.

"Why did they do it? And who are they?" Brandon shook his head then looked at the floor. Frankie waited.

"To teach me a lesson. It's all about money," Brandon said in a weak voice.

"Go on."

"I owe them a ton of money. The people I owe it to, they're..., they're ruthless, vicious. I have a gambling problem. You know how it goes. You lose then try to recoup. I'm not a stupid man, but...."

"What did you gamble on?"

"You name it I'd gamble on it, stocks, shares, horses, why I even bet a hundred grand on a snail race once. Won it too. The more speculative or crazy, the better as far as I was concerned. It was the thrill of beating the odds. Man I love that feeling, nothing like it."

"How much, how much do you owe these people Brandon?"

"About a million, give or take...."

"UK Pounds?!" Frankie asked, incredulity written on his face. "Jesus Christ Almighty. How on earth...?"

"Oh, it's easy Frankie. But don't forget, there's a whole load of compound interest in that figure, but still."

"I thought you'd married into big money."

"So did I. And it was true up to a point, but her old man, my father-in-law, he wasn't that keen on me. So, Fiona didn't get the dowry she expected, and neither did I."

"And you didn't have any money of your own? I thought you were a wealthy investment analyst, least that's what the newspaper article about your wife's death said."

"Same problem. I was good at it, I am good at it, and I did make money. But I just kept on gambling it away. It's a disease, an addiction. My father, he told me I was just like his Dad, Frank Mellor, nee Shackleton. He said I'd inherited the same destructive gambling gene. Said his father was a crazy risk taker, probably why he stole the jewels, then got into bank fraud later."

"A gambling gene?" first time I've heard that excuse," said Frankie. Brandon looked Frankie in the eye.

"It's true. Gambling is just another form of risk taking. You do it and you know there's a good chance you'll lose, but that's part of the thrill. My father said Frank's brother Ernest was the same, said he just channeled risk in a different way. Those expeditions. Hard to think of anything riskier that the things he did. You know he was only 47 years old when he died?"

"I didn't no. And I guess there might be some truth in what you say, but sounds to me like it could be a way of excusing irresponsible behavior."

"Maybe? I don't know, but it really doesn't matter anymore. I'm done." Frankie couldn't help feeling a bit sorry for Brandon, he looked totally defeated.

"So, you're saying these people you owe money to, they killed your wife?"

"Yes. They threatened me. Said something would happen, said I had no idea what they could do. The crown jewels were my last hope. I had them stashed over here for a rainy day. I reckoned I could get more money for them over here and it would be easier to hide. When all the money had gone, I still had those to cash in, but then the hurricane came and...."

"Had you hidden them in the wall?"

"Yes. Wasn't difficult and seemed safe enough.

"And when you saw the damage Irma had done, you thought someone was likely to find them?"

"I was certain they would. Might have been someone honest, but I'd still have a lot of explaining to do. For a while, it seemed as though the condos had escaped serious damage, but then the water inundated the property and then came the mold. I couldn't believe it when they said they were stripping out the condos, even the sheetrock walls. I knew the jewels couldn't possibly be missed. That someone would find them."

"Once I realized that, back in 2017, I didn't know what to do. The pressure was enormous.

I decided to remortgage the house, pay them enough to get some breathing space and give me some capital to invest."

"And what did your wife think about that?"

"She didn't know. I forged her signature to get the mortgage."

"But your investments failed?" asked Frankie.

"Yeah. I needed a high yield return and the only way to get that was to invest in high-risk stock. Profit's just reward for risk, after all. The higher the risk, the higher the return."

"Just another form of gambling then?" said Frankie. Brandon looked up as though he was about to defend his actions but then looked away and spoke.

"Yeah, you're right. It was gambling. And surprise surprise, I lost."

"Do you know who took the jewels Brandon?"

"No, I tried to find out, but I couldn't. But you obviously did." Frankie winced.

"Well, we're pretty sure we know who took them out of your condo. But we don't actually know where they are now. The guy we think took them, he died. Natural causes it's claimed."

"You bastard," said Brandon shaking his head, "you lied to me."

"Yes, I did. Doesn't make that much difference to you now though, does it Brandon?"

"I guess not. So, where do we go from here?"

"Well, you go back to the UK as you planned. Tell the police what you know about this gang. Hope they believe you, and maybe you get off the hook?"

"Doesn't make much difference, does it? Oner way or another, I am responsible for Fiona's death, aren't I? I may not have physically killed her, but if it wasn't for my stupidity, she'd still be alive."

"That's for you and your conscience to sort out." Frankie replied.

"And what about the jewels?"

"We'll try to find them and if we do, they go back to the rightful owners, the Irish state I suppose."

"Will I be in trouble for those do you think?"

"I doubt it. There may be some consequences, but as it stands, they're still missing. If they turn up, I guess the Irish authorities will be very happy and may wish to minimize the embarrassment of how they were so easily stolen. You'll have to wait and see. In the meantime, I'd get yourself busy helping the police find the killers of your wife and bring them to justice."

"Yeah, you're right. Funny those jewels. Never really been anything but a source of worry and stress for our family. Wondering where to hide them, never daring to sell them in case the trail led back to us. Good riddance is what I say."

"Okay Brandon, well good luck," said

Frankie getting up "I think you're going to need it" Brandon didn't reply, just opened the door to let Frankie out.

CHAPTER 27

PRESENT

Saturday 29 February
Frankie

Frankie got back to his condo, called detective Randazzo and reported on his meeting with Brandon Mellor.

"So, did you manage to confirm if your hunch was correct?"

"I did. I was right. And you'll love this."

"Can't wait, come on, the suspense is killing me."

"Well, you remember the story about how the Irish Crown jewels were stolen?"

"I do of course," Randazzo replied, "So?"

"See, the person they suspected to be the thief was a guy called Frank Shackleton. The younger brother of the famous artic explorer Ernest Shackleton, or to give him his full title, Sir Ernest Henry Shackleton."

"Sir Ernest Henry Shackleton, wow!" said the detective. "You limeys know how impressed us ignorant Yankees are with all those highfalutin titles."

"Yeah right. Well, it's an aside really." Said Frankie studiously ignoring the jibe. "They couldn't hang the theft on Frank Shackleton. However, his later activities suggested they were probably right to assume it was him. Some years later he was jailed for bank fraud and theft. So quite an all-round bad hat it seems, but this is the kicker. When he came out of jail he moved from Ireland to the south of England where his brother, Sir Ernest, got him a job. But by then he'd changed his name to Mellor."

"Holy shit!" exclaimed Randazzo, "they're related?"

"Looking at the dates of births, deaths ages etc., I guessed that Brandon was, well is, Frank Shackleton's grandson."

"Well, I'll be damned!" exclaimed Randazzo. That's.... I don't know what it is, but hot diggity dog!" Frankie laughed. The detective and Frankie talked some more, Frankie explaining what happened in detail and the detective asking questions.

"Does he think he's in trouble for the Irish jewels?"

"I don't think he's sure and neither am I if I'm honest. What's your take on it? Would the US police be interested, or indeed be able to prosecute Brandon for a historical crime that occurred in another country?"

"I doubt it. I'm not even sure if I should

make any kind of formal report at this time. As fantastic a result as this is Frankie, I'm not sure where it leaves us. I'm gonna have to think about this. Do we have the right, or even the legal mechanism to charge Brandon with a crime of this nature?" This is a real head scratcher. The guy who stole the jewels is long gone. Then again, I suppose Brandon could be charged with possession of stolen goods. But would the American authorities have the right? Would they be interested? My guess is not. And I'm not sure we'd even want to get involved with all the potential international implications. My guess is it would be up to the Irish authorities to take this forward."

"I think you're probably right Sam, but there is still the problem. We haven't found the stolen goods yet, have we? All we have is a picture and an uncorroborated story from Mrs. Kennedy. We do have a sort of confession from Brandon Mellor, but without solid evidence, i.e., the stolen goods themselves, I guess any decent lawyer could ride a coach and horses through that."

"You're right Frankie. "Nevertheless, well done, you were right, you smartass. And that has to be one of the oldest coldest cases in history you just solved. Look, it's the weekend so what says we leave it for now, maybe catch-up Monday?"

"Suits me," said Frankie, "Daisy's coming round for dinner tonight, so I'd better start preparing the meal." He finished the call with the Detective, then checked his watch.

CHAPTER 28

A few day previously

Ethan Hamilton

Ethan found the first day back at his travel agency hard work. No matter how conscientious his staff, they still managed to pile up a load of avoidable and unnecessary problems. *Two whole weeks lost ... just too long to be away from the office.* He was glad to be back in the driving seat. He was sure he'd got Covid, but when he got tested, he was clear on that front. But something had taken him down for a couple of weeks. Now he felt fit again, but he was coming back to a mountain of problems. He looked at the letter from the bank again and shook his head.

The others had just left for the day, leaving Ethan to lock up. He looked at the pile of bills on his desk. Business hadn't been doing great recently. A big travel company had opened a travel agency nearby. Using its superior financial strength, it was advertising all over the place, even advertising on the television with special loss making offers to tempt customers to them.

Ethan just didn't have the resources to compete with that kind of fire power and he was running out of money to pay the staff. Pretty soon he'd be unable to pay the rent. He looked at his watch, grunted, stretched and decided to call it a day. As he got up from his desk a man holding a grey backpack stepped through the door. He instantly recognized him.

"Joaquin, what the fuck are you doing here?"

"Hey Ethan, sorry about this. It's okay no one saw me man, I've been waiting outside, waiting until your staff left."

"But why are you here at all? I didn't call. Still have some stuff left. Don't use that much anyway as you well know."

"Yeah, I know, weekend warrior only. Don't know how you do it man, so much self-discipline," Joaquin shook his head.

"Yeah, well as it happens, I've decided not to do it any more Quino, even weekends. Business is going down the pan and needs my full attention. And anyway, you saw what it did to Teddy. You saw that right? Hanged himself in his bedroom. His mother found the poor fucker, Jesus...Was he one of your customers?"

"Yeah, he was." Juaquin looked down at the floor, then brought his head up. "Look I only sell the stuff. It's not my fault if someone, well you know... Look, you want to lock the door?" He asked looking back at the travel agency entrance.

"You want me to lock the door?" Ethan replied nonplussed.

"Yeah, probably better if you do," said Joaquin clearly agitated.

Ethan got up, locked the front door and came back to sit down, placed his arms on the desk and looked directly at his friend."

"Thanks Ethan, look, I know this seems all a bit well..."

"Look, cut the bullshit Quino," replied Ethan, "what's going on, what have you done?"

"We're friends, right? Known each other for what, four five years now, maybe more, right?" Quino said. "I didn't know who else to come to, who I could trust."

Ethan repeated the question.

"What have you done Quino?" Quino leaned down and moved the backpack to the side of the desk so Ethan could see the top of it, then he unbuckled the strap and opened the top. The backpack was full to the brim with bundles of cash, and as far as Ethan could tell, they were all $100 denomination notes.

***

"Jesus Christ, how much cash is in there Quino?"

"Somewhere upwards of five hundred k would be my estimate."

"Upwards, how much upwards Quino?"

Quino smiled. "Oh shit, I hope you're not going to ask me to look after this for you, are you? Because if you are, the answer's no, a great big fucking no! There's only one place you could have got your hands on that kinda money and if you've done what I think you've done..."

"Look Ethan, it's only for a short while. And you can have a decent share. I have a plan. Help me, and you can have twenty grand, no, make that fifty grand. You said your business was in trouble so, this can help, can't it?"

Ethan hesitated for a second or two..., *it would rescue my business for sure, but what happens when someone finds out, the cops, or the guy Ethan stole it from?* Ethan was far more scared of Trey Rubio than he was of the cops.

"No no no, no fucking way," said Ethan. "That guy you work for, he's batshit crazy. He'd murder someone just cos he didn't like the way they looked at him. It's him you stole it from right, Trey?" Joaquin nodded and smiled. "You must have a fuckin' death wish Quino."

"Yeah maybe, but he ain't going to know it's you holding for me, is he? Like I said, I have a plan. And you'd only be looking after it for a short time."

"Oh, a plan. Well, that's okay then."

"No, just listen. I leave the money with you. No one else I could trust like I trust you?"

"Then what?" said Ethan still thinking about how the money would get him out of the hole.

"I take some of the cash now to pay for my new ID. The guy says he'll provide me with a social security number, driving license, passport, birth certificate, the lot. The guy who does this, his docs are flawless."

"Then what?"

"You book me on a flight to, I don't know, somewhere far away. I disappear for a while, let things die down. Then I'll come back. I mean the way Trey's going, someone'll off him before too long. He's got more enemies than Martin Shkreli."

"Who?"

"He's the guy..., oh never mind. Look, you take the money, take your share right away if you want. Stash the rest in a locker, no big deal, right? I'll get my new ID then you book me on a flight. Then I disappear where Trey will never find me. I mean, how can he find me if I no longer exist? Foolproof right? You know I got no wife, no kids, no parents, no family to threaten. I'm bulletproof."

"What about me, he can come after me?"

"How so? I told you, he hardly knows you, doesn't know you're my friend. You're nowhere on his radar. Far as he's concerned, you don't exist."

"You sure about that?"

"I'm positive."

"So, what's your new name, ID whatever?"

"I don't know my new name yet. I've already

had my picture taken. The guy did all that stuff this morning. Once I leave the money with you, I'll go to collect the new papers, passport etc., pay the man the rest of his money. I shouldn't be gone for much more than a few hours, the guy promised and he's a top professional, so...?"

Ethan was frightened, but the thought of fifty thousand dollars..., *boy would that help me now...*

"Does Trey know the money's missing yet?"

"No man, that's why I chose now. He's gone to Vegas for a few days. Met a new chick, hired a private jet to impress her."

"If I agree to all this, where do you want to fly to under this new identity?"

"The destination don't matter. Anywhere, Europe, South America, well providing it's not Venezuela or Columbia. Maybe Australia? Always liked the idea of Australia. Somewhere reasonably safe anyway. Once I'm there I can figure out where to go next. The important thing is, I'll need to leave on the first available flight. Soon as I get my new papers and I know my new name, I'll call you. You get working on a ticket to get me out of here while I'm on my way back to you. When I go, I'll take a couple hundred grand with me and leave the rest with you. You take your fifty and put the rest in one of those storage lockers. I'll contact you once I'm settled somewhere. Later, I'll call you and we can discuss how I get the rest of my money."

"Maybe you could come on vacation to see me

and bring it? I'm not going to need all that dough for a while, and I don't want to risk taking all that with me now anyway. So, Ethan, fifty grand for staying late, booking me on a flight somewhere nice, and hiring a storage locker. How bad a deal is that?"

CHAPTER 29

PRESENT

Saturday 29 February 2020
Dinner Daisy & Ethan

Frankie had bought the ingredients to make a Catalan Fish Stew for Daisy, and she said she was going to stay over. *Wonder if I have time for an hour's fishing down at the pier?* Frankie decided he had and went downstairs to get his fishing gear out of the storage locker and put it in his car trunk. His cell ran as he was getting in the car.

"Hi Daisy, you'd better not be calling to cancel dinner. I'm cooking one of your favorites tonight and I've also got some interesting news about Brandon Mellor."

"Okay sounds fascinating. When you say one of my favorites, you mean one of your favorites don't you?" Daisy said.

"Okay, well let's say one of our favorites, plus lots of wine, and who knows what else might be on the menu?"

"Men! All they ever think about is food and sex."

"Whoa..., I'm not that shallow... I think about fishing as well," Frankie replied. Daisy laughed.

"So, been developments then, with Mellor?"

"Yeah, I'll tell you all about it over dinner. Why are you calling though?" asked Frankie.

"Well, it's just that I could do with coming round to see you this a bit earlier. Get something out of the way before dinner. How about six?"

"Sounds ominous, should I be worried?"

"No Frankie, nothing to do with you and me. It's about..., well I'd like to explain when I'm there."

"Give me a clue, I don't like surprises Daisy."

"Honestly, it's nothing to worry about. Just let me explain when I'm there okay?" Frankie checked his watch, *that's the fishing plan out the window....*

"No problem Daisy, see you at six."

Frankie decided to get dinner ready early so he could concentrate on whatever it was Daisy wanted to discuss. He assembled the ingredients for his Catalan Fish Stew.

He roughly chopped up some onion, then a large fennel bulb, poured some olive oil into a deep skillet and chucked in the chopped vegetables with some diced chorizo sausage, small chili chopped, ground fennel seeds, two crushed garlic cloves, some sweet paprika, couple of dried bay leaves and some thyme then let the vegetables soften before adding a tin of plum tomatoes, followed by some hot fish stock infused with saffron, a glug of white wine. He put a lid on and left it to simmer over a medium heat. He'd add the pieces of white fish, peeled shrimp, clams and mussels a few minutes before they were due to eat.

Frankie cut some wedges of lemon to serve with the stew, put them on one side, then prepared a salad of blue cheese, pear, arugula and walnuts. He'd add the oil and vinegar dressing later. The salad went in the fridge. Then he put two bottles of Californian chardonnay in the fridge along with a half-bottle of Mumms champagne.

He cleaned up the kitchen, set the table, tidied up his bedroom, then took Charlie for a walk around Venetian Bay. Frankie got back just in time to shower and change.

Daisy arrived at Frankie's condo prompt at six. They hugged and kissed warmly. Frankie took this as a good sign.

"Want a drink yet or would you prefer to wait?"

"Can we wait? This shouldn't take long."

"Let's sit at the coffee table," said Frankie. They walked over and sat down opposite one another. Daisy began.

"Okay, well first, you're thinking why didn't I want to talk about this over dinner?" Frankie raised his eyebrows and inclined his head in agreement, "well, it's because I thought it best to tell you about this now and not spoil the meal. I mean I guess we might still talk about it later, but I don't know, just didn't feel right. Not making much sense, am I?"

"Not so far Daisy. Why don't you just cut to the chase and tell me what this is all about."

"Okay, you know I don't have much family now, but I do have a nephew Ethan, remember?"

"Yes, you mentioned him before. The guy who owns Redwood Travel. Like I said, I met him a couple of times when I booked some flights home, very professional guy and a nice person to deal with."

"Right, well I'm worried about him. He's a good guy. Had some iffy friends as a kid and could have gone bad, but he didn't and I'm proud of him for that. He had a rough time growing up. My mom's sister, she was a disaster. She moved to Chicago, hooked up with some pretty crap guys by all accounts. She eventually married this loser, mom said, and got pregnant with Ethan."

"As soon as she had Ethan, the guy blew. She never saw him again. Then apparently, she started on the booze and drugs and Ethan was taken into care then adopted. As luck would have it, the family who took him in lived in Tampa, so we got to see Ethan some. He worked in a travel agency in Tampa but wanted to move to Naples. I guess he wanted to be near to the only family he had left, so he managed to get a job as manager of Redwood Travel.

Eventually the guy who owned it retired. He really liked Ethan, so he let him take it over for not much money. Ethan was happy as a clam for a while, business was good and then lately, some competition moved in, and his business started to struggle, really struggle."

"That's tough, and don't take this the wrong way, but what has all this got to do with me, or us?"

"Nothing directly, but well, and I know you have quite a lot on your plate at the moment, but I don't know who else I can ask about this. You might be able to help, you know offer some advice, I really don't know Frankie. I just thought..."

"Why do I get the feeling I'm going to regret uttering the next few words? But here goes. Come on Daisy, just tell me what this is all about and we'll go from there."

"I really don't want to drag you into this, especially after your recent experiences, but I didn't know who else to turn to. I mean, you're an expert in this sort of stuff."

"What 'sort of stuff' might that be?"

"You know criminal activity, that sort of thing."

"Daisy, I'm a partner in a UK security firm, we provide security, find missing people, sometimes investigate fraud and all that sort of thing. And okay, I've been getting involved in stuff over here lately that is a bit beyond my normal activities, but outright criminal activity?"

"Well, you didn't do too badly with the murders at this place, did you? You almost single handedly brought the killers to justice." Daisy reached down and took a folded newspaper out of her bag.

"Yes, but that was more by good luck than any kind of expertise." Frankie replied, "and if you remember, it nearly cost me my life."

"You're right Frankie, I'm sorry I shouldn't have... look just forget it. None of your business," said Daisy as she bent down to return the newspaper to her bag. Frankie sighed.

"Come on, what's in that newspaper Daisy? Come on, give."

Daisy retrieved the newspaper and gave it to Frankie who unfolded it on the table to reveal the headlines.

Violent Murder in Naples Suburb!! the headlines screamed. Frankie read on 'Police are reporting that a young man, Joaquin Martinez, was found dead in his Naples apartment last Monday. Police are appealing to anyone for information on the dead man who was brutally stabbed to death in what appeared to be a drug related crime. A police spokesperson said that Martinez was suspected of being a drug dealer and that his apartment had been ransacked in the course of the commission of the violent murder.'

Frankie had read enough.

"This was just yesterday. And what exactly has this to do with your nephew?"

"Yeah, well this is where it gets tricky. The people who killed this guy, they were probably looking for money, as in cash."

"And you know that how?"

"Ethan has it."

"What!?" said Frankie. "How..., I mean you're telling me Ethan's a drug dealer?"

"No, no. He might smoke the odd spliff now and then, but hard drugs, no. He's just not like that. His involvement was just by accident."

Daisy went on to tell Frankie the story of Joaquin going to see Ethan and asking him to look after some money briefly while he went to get his new identity papers, then to book him on a flight in his new identity. And how Joaquin never came back.

Frankie stopped her and asked.

"And you say this Joaquin stole the money from his drug dealer boss?"

"Yes."

"Wow! When was this?"

"A couple of days ago."

"Okay, so he agreed to look after the bag for a while, and then?"

"Well, he sat there waiting for Joaquin to return, but like I said, he never came back."

"What on earth was he thinking?"

"The guy offered Ethan $50k just to look after

the money for a couple of hours, then book him on a flight out of the country and stick the rest in a storage locker, till things cooled down and he could come back to collect it. Ethan needed the money. His business was in big trouble. And he didn't think it was much of a risk. He thought if things went wrong, he reckoned he could plead ignorance and just tell the police he was simply carrying out his client's instructions."

"But in the meantime, someone murdered this Joaquin guy? Presumably the people he stole the money from?"

"Seems a reasonable assumption, yes," Daisy replied.

"Okay, so, the solution is quite straightforward. Ethan calls the cops and tells them he has the money and wants to give it to them, but, for obvious reasons, he wants them to guarantee his anonymity. Or maybe he could call the cops and tell them the story without saying who he is, but tell them where they can pick the money up?"

"He doesn't trust the cops."

"Okay, well find a way of contacting the 'drug lord' then", said Frankie using air quotes "and tell him where he can collect the money stolen from him. If Ethan gives it back, then why would they come after him. Probably his best bet thinking about it."

"I agree and that's what I suggested."

"I sense a *but* coming."

"You sense right. He took some of the money.

Ethan took some of the money I mean."

"Then tell him to put it back. Look if it isn't too much and he's blown it on something, I might be able to help out. I've got some money put by for a rainy day."

"That's really kind off you Frankie, but I'd have loaned him the money myself if I could, but it's $50k he's taken."

"Don't tell me he's blown that kind of money in a few days? he couldn't have surely?"

"No, he didn't well sort of. He paid off his loan to the bank. They were about to pull the plug on his business, so he paid it into the bank, so now he can't get it back."

Frankie shook his head.

"I was thinking," Daisy continued, "the police won't know how much was left with Ethan in the first place, so suppose he gives it to them, explain what happened and then he's done the right thing, well almost. What do you think?"

"Good plan. Except the cops aren't that stupid. They'll ask him if he took any of the money and when he says no, then they'll probably check a few things out. Search his apartment, try to find out if he made any obvious expensive purchases recently, or deposited money in his bank account. You know, the obvious things. Come on Daisy, the likelihood of him standing up to the sort of pressure he'd be subjected to...." Daisy looked disappointed and distraught. Frankie backtracked a bit.

"I guess he could try what you suggested, but then if they found out he lied, they'd throw the book at him."

"You're right I suppose," said Daisy nodding her head and frowning. Then she looked up. "What about you telling your Detective friend Randazzo the whole story? He'd listen to you. Maybe you could persuade him to give Ethan a break?"

Frankie stroked his chin while he considered her suggestion.

"Possible I suppose. Let me think on that Daisy. Look, are you still hungry?"

"I could eat a horse," said Daisy, standing up from the table. "I want to be clear Frankie, one thing has nothing to do with the other and I'm sorry to drag you into this, I.., I just thought, but it's not your responsibility."

Frankie stood and put his arms around her.

"It's okay Daisy I understand. But let's leave it for tonight, let me sleep on it and then I'll see what I can come up with..., deal?"

"Deal Frankie. By the way, did I tell you how much I love you?"

"I think you did, but I'm always happy to hear you say it again." They kissed. "Come on, I've got some very nice cold champagne begging to be drunk."

"I'm your girl Frankie, happy to help you drink it."

"Just one more thing and then we don't mention it again tonight, but I'm going to have to think of something fairly quickly now you've told me, otherwise both of us could get into serious trouble for having knowledge of a crime and withholding that information from the police."

"Hmm, yes, I hadn't thought about that. Okay, well no more on that subject. Is that Catalan Fish Stew I can smell by any chance?"

CHAPTER 30

PRESENT

Monday 2 March 2020
Daisy Randazzo & Ethan

Frankie got out early for his run. A few thoughts had occurred to him during the night. He'd found it difficult to sleep and in his waking moments, he'd thought a lot about Ethan and his dilemma, which, thanks to Daisy's revelations, was now partly his dilemma. He fed Charlie, showered, got his email correspondence out of the way, then walked out on to his lanai and called Daisy.

"Morning Frankie and thanks for a lovely weekend I really enjoyed it. Why are you calling so early?"

"Well, we managed to avoid the subject of Ethan and not let it impinge on our weekend, but now we need to discuss it. I've had a few ideas. Have you got time right now?"

"Yes," said Daisy, her tone turning more serious, "but let me call you back from somewhere a bit more private. Two ticks, okay?" Daisy called back a minute later. "Okay, I can talk."

"The only thing I can think of is for Ethan to tell the cops, more specifically, tell Detective Randazzo. Tell him everything and throw himself on his mercy."

"No Frankie, he can't do that, they'll arrest him, he would end up in jail. No. There has to be another way."

"Sorry Daisy, but there isn't. I've thought it through a million times and Ethan has to come clean."

"And if he doesn't?"

"Then I'll have to tell Randazzo what I know. I'm not prepared to lie to Sam, not even by omission. You and I are both in possession of information of a serious crime and if we withhold that, we become part of it. We're just as guilty."

"No, no Frankie, I won't let you do that." Said Daisy her voice rising in volume and trembling with anger.

"Sorry Daisy but you can't stop me."

"Listen you self-righteous bastard, what gives you the right to get my nephew into trouble? I told you that in confidence, you can't break that. I'll never forgive you if you carry out your threat." Frankie tried to stay calm. One wrong word and he might lose her forever.

"I'm not the one who got him into trouble, he got himself into trouble when he took that money. He had a choice, and he made the wrong one. Apart from anything else, I'm not going to ruin my relationship with Sam Randazzo. He'd never trust me again. We have to tell him for Ethan's sake."

"So, what is it with you and that detective, some kind of bromance? Repressed feelings?" He could tell that Daisy was on the verge of tears now.

"That's uncalled for and you know it. If you can just hear me out. If we don't do the right thing now, this will just get worse for Ethan. He might get away with it for a while, but it'll come back to bite him and bite him bad. If he faces up to things now, we might be able to salvage something. Don't forget, you asked me to help Daisy and I'm sorry if you don't like what I'm saying, but you know I'm right."

"Daisy, are you there?" She was gone. "Shit," said Frankie. Charlie came over to him and rubbed against his leg. "Well, I really did a great job of persuading her didn't I boy?" Come on let's go for a walk. At the magic word Charlie's tail wagged and he did a little twirl. Ten minutes into the walk Frankie's cell buzzed. He looked at the screen, Daisy.

"Frankie?"

"Yes."

"I'm calling to apologize."

"No need, I get it."

"No, you're right. He fucked up and he has to face up to it. I called Ethan and spoke with him. He's crapping himself. Says the guy Quino stole from is completely insane. Say this Trey character won't hesitate to kill hm if he finds out he has his money, and he says he will find out. He wants to go to the cops, but he's afraid. Afraid of the cops and afraid of going to jail, He says Trey has people inside and will have him killed anyway."

"Look Detective Randazzo is coming to see me later. Let me talk to him. I have an idea. Maybe we can get a deal for Ethan. If he can give the cops something on Trey, then maybe they'll go easy on him. I don't know what he can do, but I trust Randazzo. Are you okay with me going ahead and telling him?"

"Yes, I am Frankie and I'm really sorry, I didn't mean those things I said."

"It's okay Daisy I understand."

"Are we still all right Frankie? I'll understand if you want to think about things, our relationship, I..."

"No, Daisy we're still okay. A few harsh words aren't going to destroy the feelings for you. Anyway, who else would tolerate me?"

"There is that," said Daisy laughing. "Let me know what he says, as soon as you can Frankie. Ethan's getting pretty desperate, he just wants to run."

"Tell him stay calm and I'll get back to you ASAP."

Later that morning, Frankie heard the

doorbell chime. Charlie rushed to the door waiting to greet whoever had come to visit. Ever optimistic it would be someone who would make a fuss of him. Randazzo had called earlier to say he was on his way. Frankie opened the door and let the detective in. Randazzo and Charlie engaged in mutual greetings. Then they went to sit on the lanai.

"Your pooch is one friendly little guy," said Randazzo taking a seat. "Just so happy all the time." Charlie was now lying on his back offering his tummy up for a tickle. Randazzo obliged.

"I'll go get coffees," said Frankie. He returned, put the coffees down and took the seat on the other side of the coffee table on the lanai.

"So, did Brandon turn himself in okay?" Asked Frankie once he'd sat down.

"He did. He'd contacted the guy investigating his wife's murder, Detective Mitchell, in advance. Gave him his flight details, so they met him off the plane and took him straight to their HQ. There was an email from Mitchell to our man who went to meet with Brandon. He thanked us for our help and cooperation. He was also grateful for the report of your conversation with Mr. Mellor. Asked me to pass on his gratitude." Frankie nodded.

Detective Randazzo drank some of his coffee gazing out over the bay.

"Great view," remarked Randazzo, "so relaxing."

"Yeah, I was lucky to find this place. South facing rear garden, so gets the sun all day on the pool." They were both quite for a couple of minutes looking out over the bay and sipping their coffees.

"So," said Randazzo, give me the blow-by-blow details of your meeting with Brandon." Frankie obliged. When he'd finished, the detective said.

"I guess the development with Brandon Mellor kind of eliminates Kellerman from involvement in the Irish crown jewels, don't it? I'm assuming they weren't collaborating in any way?"

"I very much doubt it. My feeling is Kellerman has much bigger fish to fry. He wouldn't get involved in a one off like that. If he is involved with stolen German artwork, as our German friend Becker clearly believes, even the Irish Crown Jewels pale into insignificance by comparison with the potential worth of the Nazi illegal hoard of treasures."

"Yeah, I can see that. So, Kellerman's a dead end?"

"Maybe not quite." Randazzo looked over at Frankie just as he was about to take a sip of his coffee. He smiled.

"I knew you had something. I could tell. Come on Frankie."

"Just a hunch, a feeling. But when I talked to Otto about something of value going missing in the aftermath of Irma, I could see he was surprised, mildly shocked maybe? He recovered quickly enough, but jewelry wasn't what he'd been expecting me to say, I can tell you that much."

"You any idea what he was expecting, a missing Vermeer, a rolled-up Monet maybe?"

"Nah, come on be serious. No, if I was to guess, it would be mazuma, filthy lucre, greenbacks, folding stuff...."

"Yeah, okay, I get it," said the detective laughing.

"Becker thinks Kellerman is somehow selling paintings stolen and hidden by the Nazis. Well, more to the point, by Kellerman's father, General Heinric Kellerman. Selling them over here in America."

"And do you think that what he's doing? That's where this mystery cash came from?"

"I don't actually."

"You don't? Come on Frankie you're talking in riddles. If the imaginary hidden cash didn't come from selling illegitimate paintings, where did it come from?"

"Don't know exactly. I have an idea. But I don't want to say what it is until I've worked on it a bit more. Might take me a week or so, but no rush. I heard on the grapevine the Kellermans have gone cruising again, be back in a week or so."

"You going to run your theory past the German detective, this Becker guy?"

"Might do, once I've done a bit more research, then I might call or email him and try my theory out on him."

"You want to share it with me now Frankie.?"

"If you don't mind Sam, let me try it out on him first."

"Sounds intriguing, let me know."

"Will do Sam, let's see how it pans out first. You in a hurry by the way?" Sam looked at his watch, "I'm okay for a while, why?"

"Want another coffee then?" The detective said he would, screwing his eyes up and looking at Frankie.

"Do I smell trouble Frankie?"

"I'm not sure, let me get a couple of refills then I'll try to explain." Frankie came back a couple of minutes later with the coffees.

"There's something I'd like to run by you, well ask you a few questions really."

"Fire away Frankie."

"Before I begin, I just want to say that I understand you can't keep this confidential. That you'll have to act on it, but I'm hoping we can strike some sort of deal. I don't know how it works, but..." The detective looked over his coffee cup at Frankie.

"You never fail to surprise me Frankie. So, what is it we can do a deal on, I'm fascinated." Frankie drew in a big breath and began the tale

Daisy had told him about Ethan. Randazzo interjected on occasion to get clarification on some point, but largely remained silent. Frankie finished telling the story, then added.

"So, what I was wondering is, could Ethan get some sort of deal if the information he provides, puts this major drug supplier away? Would he still be charged and have to serve time? Obviously, he doesn't' want to go to jail, but what really scares him is that this Trey, who he is sure has contacts in prisons, will have him killed anyway."

"Unfortunately, he's probably right to think that. And the answer to your question is, it's a possibility. If he comes clean, tells us everything, and we're able to use that information to bring down a big drugs gang, then he might walk, might even qualify for witness protection. But it's not up to me. I can make my views known, but this sort of stuff is out of my hands. My advice to Ethan though, is, it's probably the only chance he's got. He's in serious danger if what you've told me is correct."

"What do we do next?"

"Bring him down to headquarters. But we need to get him in with as few people as possible knowing. I'd like to think all Naples police department personnel are squeaky clean, but there's bound to be some of them on the make. The less people that know, the better at this stage."

"I'll talk to him, well I'll talk to Daisy and get her to talk to him, then I'll call you, if that's okay?"

"Okay Frankie," said Randazzo getting up to leave. "I'll wait for your call. In the meantime, I'll have to inform my boss about this, you understand?" Frankie nodded and showed Randazzo out.

CHAPTER 31

PRESENT

Tuesday 3 March
Ethan & Frankie and Trey

After Randazzo had left, Frankie called Daisy, but she wasn't answering her phone, so he left a message, telling her he needed some time to relax and was going fishing, then went down to his locker and loaded his fishing gear in the trunk of his car. He drove to Naples pier. Finding a parking place wasn't too much of a problem and pretty soon he was fishing off the end of the pier and chewing the fat with the rest of the fishermen and women, a number of whom he knew to talk to from many previous visits.

There was a slight breeze, and the sea was at full tide, so promising conditions for catching some fish. Frankie was soon absorbed in the fishing and caught a large pompano which was a keeper for dinner for tomorrow. A Spanish mackerel run came along and all the fishermen had great sport for half an hour, then it subsided but still quite a few fish were caught. Frankie suddenly realised he'd been there for well over an hour and still hadn't heard back from Daisy.

He bid his fishing friends farewell and headed back down the pier to where his car was parked. Throwing his tackle in the trunk he sat in the car and looked to see if there were any messages on his phone. It was switched off. He realised he'd been on auto pilot and switched it off when he got to the pier. He always turned off his phone when he went fishing off the pier. One, to not be bothered while he was trying to relax or be distracted when playing a fish, and two, to avoid annoying the other fishermen.

"Shit!" he said and turned his cell back on. It dinged immediately to signify a text message.

Frankie where are you, Ethan's having some sort of breakdown I need you D xxx Frankie called her. She answered on the first ring.

"Frankie, thank God. Ethan is here with me at my condo. He had a warning from someone he knows, saying that Trey is looking for him, offering money to anyone who can tell him where to find Ethan. He's out of his mind with terror. Says this Trey character is crazy and if he knows that Quino left the money with him, then he's as good as dead."

"Okay, try to calm him down

. You can tell him I've spoken to Detective Randazzo. I described the situation and asked him, you know, what would happen if etc. He said he might be able to get Ethan a deal, but that would depend on a number of factors. Depends how good the Ethan's information is etc., but he said in principle, he should be able to do something. Says it wouldn't be up to him, he'd have to talk to his boss. I can call him back now and tell him it's become more urgent, and we can give him details. I assume Ethan doesn't feel he can go back to his apartment. Can Ethan stay with you?"

"I already suggested that, but Ethan says Trey might find out he could be staying with his Aunt Daisy and come looking for him at my place. I can't see how that could happen, but Ethan won't stay, won't risk putting me in danger." Frankie sighed...

"You'd better bring him to my place. I'll be back there in twenty minutes. He'll have to stay with me until we can get a deal worked out with Randazzo."

"Frankie... I can't put this on you. This isn't your nephew in trouble. Maybe he could go stay in a hotel, out of town somewhere maybe?"

"He could, but I think he might be safer staying in my condo. Anyway, that way, Randazzo can come and talk to him, see what he has to offer in return for a deal."

"I don't know what to say Frankie."

"Then don't say anything. Look it's only a couple of days. We'll get something sorted. Bring him round but be careful. Try not to let anyone see him leaving your place or coming to my condo, okay?"

"Okay Frankie and thanks for this." Half an hour after Frankie got back, the doorbell chimed. It was Daisy. Frankie opened the door and Daisy entered followed by Ethan.

"Hi Mr Armstrong, thanks, I.." Frankie put his hand up to stop him talking.

"It's Frankie, okay? and, not another word of thanks Ethan. Happy to help. Maybe you can return the favour one day. Come on, let me show you where you'll be sleeping." Ethan followed Frankie a small knapsack on his back. Frankie showed him into the spare bedroom. "Just make yourself at home, I'll show you where everything is later". Ethan started to thank Frankie again then stopped, smiled and put his knapsack on the bed.

"I'll just go talk to Daisy," said Frankie and left Ethan to settle in. Daisy was sitting stood, looking out over the bay. "I had a quick word with Randazzo just before you got here," said Frankie, "and he's coming over. He's busy on a case at the moment, but he'll be here in a couple of hours at most he says. So go Daisy and don't worry."

"Okay Frankie, you're the boss," said Daisy smiling.

"Yeah right, since when?" They kissed and she left. Frankie went to make some coffee, then went to check on Ethan. He was flat out on the bed asleep. Frankie took his coffee on to the lanai and drank it while looking out over the bay, ruminating on Ethan's situation. He drained the last of his drink, then went to sit at his computer to do some research on drugs in Florida.

Florida is one of the most beautiful and vibrant states in America. It's also susceptible to America's growing substance abuse problem.

If you live in Florida, then you've seen first-hand how drug and alcohol abuse has affected its citizens. Methamphetamine and cocaine abuse has been a storied part of South Florida's past, but the opiate crisis has begun to trickle down as well.

More and more, we're seeing good people fall victim to opioids. These drugs are incredibly dangerous and becoming available to anyone looking. Addicts come from different backgrounds and circumstances, but many of the stories end up in the same place.

If you want to keep yourself or your loved ones away from this ending, you've got to find them help. In this post, we're going to give you 7 Florida drug abuse statistics to consider when thinking about the addict(s) in your life.

Some of them may be surprising, some of them won't be, but all of them will rattle you to your core. Let's learn more about this problem.

He was just about to read more when the door chime went. Frankie checked the time. *That's' bit soon for Randazzo?* He went to the door and shouted. “Who is it?”

“Amazon delivery,” came the answer, “got to have a picture with the door open please.” Frankie was expecting an order, but he still put the chain on and began to open the door. Something akin to a freight train came hurtling through the door, ripping the chain off as it was flung open wide and sending Frankie staggering backwards. The man came in and kicked the door back closed with his foot. He was taller than Frankie and a bit broader. Big, but not fat.

The stretch white T shirt he wore revealed a hard muscular body oozing power and strength. He had long dark shiny hair pulled into a ponytail, an evil smile and eyes as hard as flint. He also had what looked like a Smith & Wesson M&P 9 in his hand and it was pointing at Frankie.

“Let’s not mess about here brother, I want the boy and I want my money.” He had a faint accent, but his words were crisp and clear.

In response to the noise, Ethan appeared at the door to the living room, took one look and fled back down the hall. The man snarled,

“You!” he shouted. Frankie, taking advantage of his momentary distraction, chopped at the man’s gun hand. The gun fell on the floor and clattered as it slid away. Frankie kicked it further away out of the man’s reach. The man smiled.

“A hero? I’m going to enjoy this,” said the man as he charged at Frankie. Frankie side stepped and with a hefty push sent the man sprawling sideways. Frankie was torn, wanting to go for the gun, but not wanting to squander his meagre advantage. The man was back on his feet in a second, *no time for the gun.* He came in close and got Frankie in a bear hug and began to squeeze. Frankie head butted him, and Trey grunted as blood spurted from his nose. Trey loosened his grip giving Frankie the chance to stick two fingers in his eyes.

The man howled with rage, backed off, then quickly recovered and charged at Frankie again. Frankie kept his calm and as the man rushed him, he chopped him in the throat, just under his chin. Trey looked shocked and put his hand to his throat making a croaking noise, but again recovered swiftly and came back at Frankie, landing a hefty punch to Frankie's solar plexus. Frankie gasped and bent over. Trey took full advantage and brought his knee up into Frankie's face. It was now Frankie's turn to spurt blood from his nose. He managed to stay upright and backed off briefly while Trey shook himself, ready to come at Frankie again.

This time Trey had obviously decided to use his reach to his advantage and adopted a boxer's stance. He pushed the easy chair out of the way with his foot to give him more room to manoeuvre and started to circle around Frankie. Frankie was an experienced boxer but was worried about getting punched in the head. His previous injury made that so much more dangerous.

Trey threw a punch. Frankie ducked and feinted. Out of the corner of his eye, he saw Ethan re-emerge from where he'd been hiding. He managed to give Ethan a brief meaningful glance then quickly looked at the gun on the floor. The brief distraction cost Frankie. Trey took advantage and threw a fast right hook. Frankie just about manged to turn his body taking the punch on his upper arm. Both men were panting, both covered in blood. They circled each other. Trey aimed a vicious kick at Frankie's groin and made contact. Frankie gasped in pain and fell to his knees. He was vulnerable now.

Frankie knew the next blow could likely be the last. He had no doubt Trey would move in to finish him and kill him without batting an eyelid. Trey stood over Frankie, confident, knowing it was almost over. Then he moved back a little to get the momentum for a final fatal kick at Frankie's head. Trey was grinning now, savouring the moment. Victory was his. Frankie prepared himself for the onslaught. Then simultaneously Trey's mouth dropped open as a deafening shot rang out. Trey half turned to look at Ethan who stood, gun wobbling in his two hands, tears running down his face as he kept the gun pointing at the big man. Trey went down like a demolished building.

*

Frankie got to his knees just as Lieutenant Detective Sam Randazzo rushed into the condo, gun drawn.

"What the fuck! said Randazzo taking in the scene and bringing his gun up to point at Ethan. Frankie put one hand up his other hand nursing his abdomen.

"No Sam... not him."

"Drop the gun on the floor." The detective shouted at Ethan who was now holding the gun down by his side. He let go of it and it fell to the floor. Randazzo moved over quickly, retrieved the gun and stuck it in his belt. He then went over to the body on the floor and checked for a pulse. Then looking at Ethan said,

"Come on man, help me get Frankie up and into that chair." Ethan seemed to snap out of his trance and came over to help. They slowly manoeuvred Frankie into one of the dining chairs. Randazzo went to the drinks cabinet and poured a large slug of scotch into a tumbler, brought it over to Frankie and held it to his lips. Frankie gulped some and leaned back. "You okay?" Randazzo asked. Frankie nodded then winced.

"Yeah, I'm okay. Battered and bruised, but okay." Randazzo got on his cell and called for an ambulance and back up. By now Ethan was sitting on one of the other dining chairs, head in his hands.

"Am I to take it that you're Ethan?" Asked

Randazzo. Ethan looked up and nodded.

"Yes."

"And did you shoot the guy on the floor there?" Ethan nodded again.

"I thought he was going to kill Mr Armstrong."

"There was no thought about it," said Frankie, "If Ethan hadn't shot that guy when he did, I'd be dead now. That by the way," he said nodding towards the prone body on the floor, "is Trey Rubio, the drugs lord that Ethan's friend stole the money from, and no doubt the same guy who also killed his friend."

"Okay, we can get into all that later. But how did this Trey know that Ethan was here?" Frankie shrugged his shoulders.

"Daisy brought Ethan so maybe he knew Ethan was with Daisy?"

"Not quite right. Daisy was going to bring me straight here, but I thought I'd better collect my car from where I'd left it parked behind the travel agency. In case I needed it later. I arranged to meet my Aunt Daisy here in the car park, then we came up together."

The detective gave Frankie a meaningful look.

"Trey had Ethan's travel agency staked out. Probably one of his minions watching the place and told to tell Trey if Ethan appeared. The guy probably followed Ethan, saw him come to your place then called it in." Ethan looked mortified.

"I'm really sorry Frankie, sorry, Mr Armstrong. I just..."

"It's okay Ethan, it worked out in the end. I think you redeemed yourself by shooting that man. Not an easy thing to do in any circumstances."

The ambulance arrived sirens wailing. Randazzo went out into the corridor which overlooked the car park and shouted directions to the medics.

CHAPTER 32

PRESENT

Sunday 1 March – 3 March
Brandon gives himself up

The Delta Airbus 350 airplane took off from Atlanta, capital of the U.S. state of Georgia, and headed north, eventually turning east to make its way over the Atlantic Ocean and onwards on its journey to London. Brandon had fallen asleep briefly as soon as the aircraft left the ground, but then woke up and looked out of the window as the aircraft flew over the coast. The light fading now as they flew into the dark night.

He reflected on his Irishness, as he always did when crossing the mighty Atlantic. Although born in England, Brandon Mellor always considered himself Irish. So many of his fellow Irishmen in the past had crossed this same huge ocean by sea, to escape famine, poverty and the tyranny of their English rulers. They knew full well the crossing by boat was perilous, but many considered the risk and dangers worthwhile, in order to have a chance to start a new life in America. In those early days, Brandon knew it could take up to twelve weeks to sail from Ireland to America. Now he'd be crossing this same vast ocean in a matter of hours.

Turning away from the window, he focused his mind on recent events. *My stupid gambling addiction, I didn't need the money, well not until I gambled and got into debt. Why the fuck did I get involved in borrowing from those people? Look where it's landed me now, on my way to get arrested for killing my wife. It was always going to end badly I knew that, but I didn't think they'd go that far, didn't think they'd kill Fiona. It was my fault my fault completely I might as well have strangled her with my own bare hands.*

"Would you like a drink sir?" The stewardess asked. Brandon didn't seem to hear. She repeated the question but this time a bit louder "Sir, would you like a drink?" Snapping out of his reverie, Brandon looked up and apologized.

"Sorry, miles away, no thanks. But could I have a blanket and a pillow please."

"Yes sir, of course."

"Oh, and please don't wake me for dinner or anything, I'll just sleep through?" added Brandon.

"As you wish sir. Madam?" she said to the woman sat next to him.

"Large G & T please," said the woman.

"Very good madam. I'll go get your pillow and blanket sir," she said nodding to Brandon. He went back to his thoughts.

"And now I could be in trouble because of my grandfather stealing those jewels. "What a fucking mess," he said out loud., The lady on his right looked way from her book and turned to stare at him. "Oh, sorry," said Brandon, "I was just thinking about something and...it slipped out, sorry" he said again. The woman said nothing, frowned and went back to her book.

"How can I make things right? thought Brandon. The stewardess brought his pillow and blanket and told the lady sat next to him she'd be along shortly with her drink. Brandon reclined his seat, made himself as comfortable as possible and as he closed his eyes a plan began to form in his mind. *Yes of course,* he said to himself, then fell asleep.

*

The aircraft landed heavily on the runway at Heathrow, jolting Brandon awake. He waited patiently until his fellow passengers had deplaned, then took down his cabin luggage and made his way slowly towards the back of the plane, out and along the airbridge and into the airport. A uniformed policeman accompanied by what Brandon assumed was a plain clothes policeman, or detective, stood by the exit obviously referring to a picture of him as they scanned the faces of the passengers coming off the airbridge.

The plain clothes man stepped forward.

"Mr. Mellor?" Brandon nodded. "My name is Detective Sergeant Wallace. Is that your only luggage?" Brandon nodded again. "I'm afraid we're going to have to handcuff you. Please hold out your arms. Sergeant, take his bags, would you?" The sergeant did as he was asked. Wallace cuffed Brandon whilst curious people looked on. "Okay, now follow me please." The police car was parked outside the terminal in a no parking zone, driver in place. They got in, Wallace and Mellor in the rear, the other two in front.

Apart from the odd brief comment about the traffic, everyone remained silent during the forty-five-minute journey to Surry Police headquarters in Guilford. When they arrived, Brandon was taken by the arm by a burley desk sergeant and shuffled off into a police cell measuring just nine feet by twelve. There was a bench bolted to one wall and a metal toilet in the corner. Brandon sat on the bench and waited. Sometime later a policeman came to ask him if he needed a drink of water. He declined the offer.

An hour and a half later a man he recognized as Detective Mitchell came along with the desk sergeant who opened the cell door.

"Follow me," said the detective and led him to an interview room where there were two other people, sergeant Wallace who was standing and a young lady in police uniform sitting on a chair at a metal table which was bolted to the floor. "Sit here please Mr. Mellor, if you would." He sat and noted the flickering tube on the overhead neon lights. "And get that fucking tube replaced Wallace, how many times do I have to ask?"

"Yes sir," said Wallace looking embarrassed. Detective Mitchell placed a folder on the desk, opened it and nodded at the young lady who went over to a recording device on a shelf and pressed a couple of buttons. Detective Mitchell stated the date and time and those present. He then proceeded to formally charge Brandon with the murder of his wife. He asked if he understood the charges and asked him if he wanted a solicitor present.

"No," said Brandon.

"So, said Mitchell, "Did you kill your wife?"

"No, I didn't," said Brandon. "But I can tell you who did." The detective inclined his head as in a 'really?' gesture, looked at the others and smiled.

"Okay, well this should be interesting. You want to tell us who, and perhaps more pertinently, why?" Brandon told them the whole story, leaving nothing out. The gambling the borrowing, remortgaging the house, everything.

"Wow," said Detective Mitchell, when Brandon came to the end of his story. "I suppose all that makes sense. So, this Branko Subotic, you think he killed your wife?"

"I don't think, I know."

"How?"

"He told me, he called me and told me. The day he did it. I didn't believe him. I thought he was just trying to scare me. I rushed home and... I should have known better."

"Why didn't you tell us this before?"

"I.. I don't know. Maybe a mixture of shame and fear." The detective nodded his head.

"And that's why you didn't want to post a reward. You didn't want us to find him?"

"Yes." Brandon replied.

"And these jewels these Irish Crown Jewels. Detective Randazzo mentioned them to me. Not that I'm over interested in those at the moment, but you want to tell me about that? Do they have any relevance in relation to our wife's death?"

"No," said Brandon. "No, no relationship at all to Fiona's death."

"Okay, so I assume you'd be willing to identify this," the detective looked at his notes, "this Branko Subotic? Pick him out of a lineup, make a witness statement, testify in Court if we can catch him and charge him?"

"No, I wouldn't."

"You scared of this character? We can protect you if what you say is true, and we can prove it."

"I'm not scared of him. Maybe I was, but I'm not now. It's just that I don't think that approach would do any good. He'd find a way of getting away with it. After all, it would be just my word against his, wouldn't it?"

"Unless we can get concrete proof, probably." said the detective.

"Okay," said Brandon. "Maybe I have a better idea then. First, you need to take me to my home to get my car, then let me make a phone call."

"Your car?"

"Yes, he knows my car." The detective thought for a couple of seconds.

"You mean to arrange to meet him, don't you?"

"I do. Maybe I can get him to admit it or say something incriminating. I mean that stuff about wearing a wire to trap people, it isn't just stuff in the movies, is it?"

After several attempts to call Branko Subotic, Brandon finally got past two of his minions, and spoke directly to him. He asked Subotic if they could meet the next morning.

"You have the money?"

"I have nearly four hundred thousand in cash, if you're interested?" He heard Branko talking to his men in Serbian or whatever it was. He came back on the line.

"Meet me at the Virginia Water car park. Just off London Road. You know where it is?"

"Yeah, I do," said Brandon.

"Be there at 11:30 a.m., got it? Any funny business and you'll be joining your wife." Brandon winced. "You still have the same car?" the man continued.

"I do and I'll be there at 11:30 on the dot."

Brandon persuaded Mitchell to let him stay the night in his own house, with Wallace keeping him company. Wallace didn't look too thrilled, but Mitchell agreed, with the proviso he also put a patrol car outside the gates.

*

Next day

"So, do I have to switch anything on?" asked Brandon.

"No, it's on all the time, speech activated. All you have to do is make sure he doesn't know you're wired up."

"Supposing he asks me to remove my shirt.?"

"Then, we're sunk. But why would he suspect you're wired?"

"Because he's one smart guy. He hasn't survived this long by being a gullible fool."

"Well, if he does find out, we'll be near enough to move in and arrest him. If you're telling the truth, and he did kill your wife, then we should be able to prove it somehow. The fact that he's agreed to meet proves a prior relationship. We recorded your phone call to him, so that'll help. Anyway, let's cross that bridge if we have to," said Detective Mitchell. "How long have we got before you meet him?" Brandon checked his watch,

"Over an hour."

"Okay, well, we'll go and get the van in position and the backup cars. Wallace will follow you at a discreet distance and park where he can see you."

"And get to me, if I decide to run off?" said Brandon.

"There is that," said the detective, "is that what you're planning to do?"

"No, I'm going to nail this vicious bastard," replied Brandon grimly."

"Well, I wish you luck. I've looked into this character's record, and we've had him in custody a few times, suspected of various crimes, murder even. But we've never managed to convict him of anything serious. I think he only did jail time the once, for extortion."

The man had finished taping the wire to his body and Brandon now had his shirt and jacket back on. The man walked over to the van, opened the rear door then said, "recite Humpty Dumpty or say the alphabet, whatever, but keep talking while I test the signal." Brandon complied. The man leaned out of the back of the van and gave a thumbs up.

"You ready?" the detective said to Brandon.

"As ready as I'll ever be." He replied. Then addressing both Brandon and Wallace, Mitchell said,

"Give us about twenty minutes before you set off, okay?" They both nodded and Wallace set the timer on his phone. "We all clear on what we're doing?" Brandon and Wallace both nodded. Mitchell went over to the van, banged on the back doors. They opened and he got in, taking one last backwards glance at Brandon he shouted. "Good luck!" then got in, and the van sped away.

"I'll wait in my car if you don't mind," said Brandon and got into his car. Wallace went to his and did likewise. Brandon checked he had everything he needed, then checked again. *All set you bastard. I'm coming for you Branko Subotic.* He breathed deeply in and out. Then sat there, a solitary tear rolled down his cheek. "I love you Fiona," he said out loud, then wiped the tear away with the back of his hand and prepared for the task in front of him.

Brandon arrived at the carpark on the dot of 11:30. It was quite empty. He couldn't see Wallace's car, nor the surveillance van. He got out to stretch his legs. Branko Subotic and two of his men seemed to materialize out of nowhere.

"You can't see him," said Subotic, "but one of my men is over there with a powerful rifle pointing at your chest." Brandon followed Subotic's gaze and looked at a small clump of trees just beyond the car park perimeter. "You understand?" Brandon said he did. Detective Mitchell was in the van with two others. All of them had earphones on.

"You getting this?" Mitch said to the others. They both gave him the thumbs up. "Shit, we didn't think about a sniper. This guy is smarter than we thought." The next words out of Subotic's mouth made Mitchell even more distressed. "Oh shit," he said, as he heard the man say.

"We need to check you for a wire, Subotic said to Brandon, "hold up your arms."

"No, you don't need to check," said Brandon, "I am wearing a wire."

"What the fuck?" exclaimed Mitchell, what on earth is he playing at?" Looking through his binoculars. He saw the quizzical look on Subotic's face, then Subotic was thrown violently backwards as the shot rang out. Subotic fell to the ground and lay stock still. Mitchell raised his binoculars again to look at Brandon. Brandon was just standing there, holding the gun down by his side. Everyone seemed frozen to the spot.

Mitchel lowered his binoculars. Then another shot rang out, but a different noise this time. Mitchell raised his binoculars again and saw the spreading bloom of blood appear on Brandon's chest. Brandon looked down at his chest, then leaned back and looked up at the sky, opened his arms wide and seemed to be smiling as he fell forwards, spread-eagled out on the floor.

By now, back up police vehicles were converging on the scene, screeching to a halt, officers disgorging from the cars, guns in hand, shouting at the remaining two men. Subotic's men both put their guns on the ground and held up their hands. Wallace came running over to detective Mitchell.

"S'cuse my French, but what the fuck just happened?" he said to Mitchell. Mitchell stood there in silence looking over at the scene where two men lay dead on the ground, police herding the other two men away. "Mitch, you okay?"

"Yeah, I'm okay."

"You going to tell me why this all went tits up?"

"Oh, I don't think it did go tits up Wallace. I think it all went according to plan. It just wasn't our plan." Wallace looked at Detective Mitchel trying to work out what he meant. "Better call for the scene of crime guys Wallace, see you back at the station."

CHAPTER 33

PRESENT

Wednesday 4 March 2020

Ethan and his statement

Sitting in an interview room at Naples Police headquarters were Lieutenant Detective Sam Randazzo, Detective Sergeant Sue Thomas and Ethan Hamilton. Randazzo started the tape, named all the people present, then stated the date and time. He began by saying,

"We're recording this interview. A transcript of it will be made available to you for you to sign as your formal statement. You understand all this Ethan?" Ethan nodded. "You have to say yes for the tape."

"Sorry, yes I understand."

"Okay. I'm going to ask you once again for the tape, do you want a lawyer present at this interview?"

"No thanks," said Ethan.

"Okay, so tell your story from the beginning, your previous association with Joaquin Martinez and anything that happened in the recent past that you consider pertinent to the matter in hand. Understood?"

"Yes, I understand." So, Ethan began his story ending up with his shooting of Trey Rubio. Detective Thomas got up from her chair and switched the recoding machine off.

"Thank you for that Ethan. Anything you want to ask me?"

"Yes. Am I going to be arrested? I mean for the money and for shooting Trey?"

"I'm working on that. I don't want to give you false hope, but you have been instrumental at potentially breaking up a huge drugs wholesaling business in south Florida and beyond. So that has to count for quite a lot. The authorities are probably going to want you to testify in Court, so my guess they'll let the money thing slide. As for the shooting, no issue there. You won't be charged for anything to do with that. In fact, they might give you a medal." Ethan laughed at that. Randazzo continued. "Can't really see it any other way. I didn't say this okay? but I very much doubt you'd be charged with anything at all."

"And, if by any chance some hardass gets involved and is not willing to offer you witness protection, then just refuse to testify unless they do. But I very much doubt it wll come to that." Ethan nodded and looked relieved.

"I guess you got the money out of the storage place?"

"We did."

"Out of interest, how much was there?"

"Got it here," and the detective looked at a sheet of paper. "$765,000," he
said. Ethan whistled and said, "Wow,"

"Small change for Trey Rubio," said Randazzo, "He is, or more accurately, he was, a major league player in the drugs business in the US. A wholesaler for the Colombian drug cartel. He supplied dealers' way beyond Florida. He sure couldn't let anyone get away with stealing money off him. Wouldn't be a good look, would it? And anyway, he probably welcomed the excuse to kill someone. The guy was a homicidal psychopath. Lord only knows how many people he's killed?"

"The drug squad subsequently organized raids on all his premises and found a huge amount of evidence. Ledgers on deals, records of places and companies he used to launder cash, accounts, the works. Why you're virtually a folk hero Ethan, at least amongst the drug squad and the police community at large. The guy who killed Trey Rubio. They might even sing songs about you. Wouldn't that be a blast?"

*

The detective left police headquarters and drove to Acadiana to see Frankie. Frankie had called him when he'd got back home from the hospital.

"Hey," said Randazzo when Frankie opened the door. "Look at the state of you. I think you'd have fared better fighting Mike Tyson. At least he'd have had gloves on."

"Don't make me laugh detective, it hurts. Having said that it hurts regardless."

"They said you were okay, didn't need to keep you in?"

"They wanted to keep me in for observation but said there were no obvious serious injuries. Nothing broken, just cuts and bruises, nothing that won't heal by itself in time. They gave me some powerful pain killers. So here I am. How'd it go with Ethan?"

"Statement made, so all good. I've dropped him off at a safe house where he can stay until he's sorted out with the wit protection program."

"So, no problem with that, no criminal charges for the money or anything?"

"A few details to iron out," said the detective, "but I'll make sure he doesn't face any charges. That guy did everyone a favour when he pulled the trigger."

"He certainly did me one, that's for sure," Frankie replied.

"He sure did," said Randazzo, "but that's not the end of it."

"How d'you mean?"

"I've been talking to the Chief about the money."

"You mean a budget for my time and A&B Security?"

"No, Frankie, sorry I forgot all about that. I promise I'll get that sorted. No, I meant the money the guy dumped on Ethan, that money."

"What about 'that' money?" said Frankie, emphasising 'that'.

"We don't know who it belongs to," said the detective. Frankie pulled a face.

"Didn't it belong to Trey Rubio?"

"Yeah, well maybe theoretically, but he's dead. And I don't think anyone's going to be trying to claim the proceeds of selling illicit drugs on behalf of his estate, do you?"

"I suppose not," said Frankie looking perplexed.

"I know, it's a weird one. And yes, we do know it's almost certainly the proceeds from selling illicit drugs etc etc. But the truth is, we can't know for sure, can we?"

"So?"

"Well, it's kind of in limbo. We don't have anyone to give it back to, do we?"

"I guess not. But can't you give it to a charity or something, or maybe the police benevolent fund?" Randazzo gave Frankie a hard look. "No, I didn't mean it like that!"

"Yeah, I know Frankie, just funnin with you. No, the truth is, the last person we know it belonged to, is Ethen. The guy who gave it to him is also dead, so..."

"What!? You're not telling me Ethan gets to keep the money? I don't believe it." Randazzo shrugged his shoulders.

"Maybe... the chief thinks it's more than likely. He's taking advice, but he had something similar in the past... and he thinks that's what's going to happen. But don't say anything to anyone about it just yet, but who knows? Looks likely. It's a funny old-world Frankie."

"Jesus Christ Almighty." Frankie said.

"Yeah, him too. Well, Frankie, you just take it easy and let me know if you need anything. Have a rest, sit by the pool and relax some." Frankie was still shaking his head.

"Okay," he replied, "but I'm not too good at that. Anyway, I've been thinking about the Kellermans and their little cruises around the Caribbean islands. I went on one once, four or five days. Very enjoyable, but long enough for someone like me who gets bored after a week at sea."

"You planning to go and talk to Otto some more?"

"I am. Not today for sure, but soon yeah, maybe Friday. I think I'll spend the next couple of days soaking up the sun and recharging my batteries, then I'll see how I'm feeling. I have some ideas about what he might be up to. I'll call you and let you know when I decide to go see him."

"Okay Frankie and do as you're told, take it easy and rest."

"I will I promise." When Randazzo left, Frankie went to get a beer, but then the ideas he'd been ruminating on, crystalized in his mind. He forgot the beer, went to sit at his PC and got to work researching specialist photography techniques and other related matters. After an hour's research he went to the lanai and sat down re-reading the notes he'd made. *That's got to be it!* He decided to call Karl Becker. He looked at his watch. It was late afternoon in Germany. He called the number Becker had given him and was told Detective Becker had gone home already and he wouldn't be available for a few days as he was in Court for the rest of the week.

"Damn," said Frankie.

"Sorry sir, what was that you said?"

"I said not to worry, thanks." He put the phone down and composed an email to the Detective outlining his thoughts and theories. He looked at it, then parked it as a draft. *I'll do some more thinking on this…*

CHAPTER 34

PRESENT

Friday 6 March 2020
Frankie and Otto Kellerman

Having spent the previous couple of days fishing and relaxing by the pool, Frankie woke up on Friday morning feeling much better. After taking Charlie for a walk, he spent the rest of the morning doing more research and became increasingly confident about his theories. He re-read the draft email he'd prepared for Detective Becker, made a couple of small alterations, then pressed send. Frankie picked up his cell and called Sam Randazzo.

"Lieutenant Detective Randazzo here. I can't talk to you at the moment so leave a message."

"Shit!" said Frankie out loud. Charlie came to sit at his feet. He didn't like it when Frankie sounded angry. "Not you Charlie," he said, ruffled the fur on Charlie's head and got a big tail wag in return. Frankie left a message for Detective Randazzo telling him what he was going to do and what action he wanted the detective to take and to call him back. After an hour, the detective still hadn't returned his call.

"Hmm, what the hell?" he said out loud and got up to go visiting. *Just hope he's home*. Frankie walked down the steps to the ground floor. As he reached the bottom of the steps, his cell buzzed. Randazzo.

"Thanks for calling back Sam. I'm just on my way there now. You okay with what I suggested? Probably being a bit over the top here, but you never know, he might just cave?"

"Yeah, okay Frankie, but take it slow, I need to get organized. Give me ten minutes at least." Frankie was keen to get going, *ten minutes wouldn't make any difference*, he thought and walked out of the Acadiana car park and up the road to the bridge overlooking the bay. He stopped at the top of the bridge and watched the boats going under, either on their way out to the Gulf or returning. After a while he checked his watch and made his way to Roman Plaza. His cell buzzed. A message from Randazzo, *on my way*.

Frankie walked through the car park, round the corner along the corridor to Otto Kellerman's condo and pressed the bell. He heard the chimes inside. Hildegard opened the door, a non-too friendly look on her face. A voice from within the said.

"Who is it Hildi?"

"That man from Acadiana, Mr..."

"Armstrong," Frankie said helpfully.

"Yes, I heard Hildi. Please let Mr. Armstrong in Liebling." She opened the door to let Frankie walk through, then closed it. Frankie's cell chirruped. He took it out of his shirt's breast pocket, looked at the screen, pressed a button and replaced it in the pocket.

"What can I do for you, Mr. Armstrong? My my, you look as if you've been fighting."

"An accident, nothing serious," said Frankie. "And please call me Frankie. May I call you Otto?" Kellerman looked uncomfortable but said,

"I suppose so. So, what exactly can I help you with, er... Frankie?"

"Well, I'm really sorry to bother you Otto, but I wondered if I could have your opinion on something? Only take a couple of minutes."

"Well, Hildi and I were just about to go shopping, but I suppose I can spare you a few minutes, please, take a seat." Frankie strolled over to a comfy looking sofa and sat down. Otto Kellerman sat on the opposite sofa.

"So, er... Frankie, how can I help you?"

"Well, you being an art expert, I thought maybe you could help. See, a friend of mine bought a painting and he thinks it might be a fake." Otto frowned and looked at Frankie. Frankie maintained his innocent face. Otto answered.

"Well, there are of course a lot of fake paintings around. But I'm not sure how I can possibly help your friend."

"It was just that he paid a serious amount of money for it and he had it examined by an expert who said it was the real thing. Do you think it's possible to fool an art expert like that?"

"Well, I wouldn't know. I mean the obvious answer is, it depends on how good the fake is. Look, I'm afraid we're going to have to go. Shopping needs to be done. You know how it is?" Frankie had memorized one of the more famous pieces of art said to have been stolen by the Nazis and never been found.

"The painting was claimed to be the Madonna with Child, painted by Lucas Cranach the Elder," said Frankie. A look of something between astonishment and horror showed on Otto's face, which was now mostly drained of color.

"Impossible!" Otto blurted out involuntarily. Frankie waited, then said.

"Impossible why? Because you know where the genuine original is?" Otto Kellerman looked shocked but managed to regain something of his previous belligerent manner.

"I.. I mean, don't be ridiculous. That painting was almost certainly destroyed in 1943 or possibly fell into the hands of the Russians," said Otto, now fully recovered.

"Or was possibly stolen by the Nazis and hidden away somewhere?" said Frankie.

"How would I know anything about that? Just because I'm German, is that what it is?"

"He thinks it was a Chinese fake." Frankie replied.

"Sorry?" said Otto.

"My friend, he thinks it's a Chinese fake," Frankie continued, "Apparently, the Chinese are absolute experts at faking paintings. I believe the really good top-notch ones can produce exact replicas that can be passed off as the real thing. Course even fakes of such quality cost a fortune, but still..." Otto was beginning to look very uncomfortable.

"Well, I feel sorry for your friend, but I'm afraid I can't help him. We really must insist you go now. As I said, we have shopping to do so..."

"D'you want to know what I think you've been up to Otto?"

"I'm sorry?" said Otto again.

"I said, d'you want to know what I think you've been up to?"

"Yes, I heard you and no, I don't, and I'm not interested in what you think. This is beyond... beyond impudence..., I insist..." At that moment Hildegard appeared from the bedroom, a pistol with a silencer on in her hand The gun barrel pointed squarely at Frankie. It didn't waver. Hildegard looked calm, confident and competent. Frankie stood and started to back away.

"No Hildi, no Liebling, put that away," Otto cried.

"So, you're going to shoot me are you Mrs. Kellerman?" said Frankie in a loud voice, "just how do you expect to get away with that?"

"We plan ahead Mr. Armstrong", she said in a heavily accented voice. "And no, we didn't expect to be caught out by a nosy neighbor in Naples, for sure. But we did think that maybe one day we'd have to run." Frankie felt the impact of the bullet before he heard the distinct phut of the silenced pistol. He dived behind the sofa. As he lay there, playing dead, he hoped she wouldn't come and finish the job. Then there was a commotion at the door, it burst open and then shots. He kept down out of the line of fire.

"You can get up now Frankie," Frankie turned over on to his back.

"Not sure I can manage that on my own Sam, the bitch shot me in the shoulder."

The detective called to his men.

"Here, help me get this guy on the sofa and call for medics, urgent!" They helped Frankie on to the sofa. He could see Otto being manhandled out of the condo. Otto was wailing in German.

"You're bleeding a lot Frankie, but doesn't look too serious," said Randazzo, "just take it easy, the medics'll be here pronto."

"Thanks Sam. Who would have thought...?"

"Yeah," said Randazzo shaking his head.

"women are often the most ruthless in these situations. Does it hurt a lot?" he asked.

"Only when I laugh," said Frankie and passed out.

Frankie came round a few minutes later to find the medics dressing his wound. Then they placed him on a gurney, jacked it up and wheeled him out of the condo and out into the car park and into a waiting ambulance. Sam got into the ambulance with the medics. The doors closed and they were off, sirens wailing as they drove away. The medic was talking to the hospital, giving them the lowdown on what to expect and what he thought they should prepare for.

"What happened to the woman, to Hildegard?" asked Frankie turning to the detective.

"Shot dead." Can't say she didn't ask for it."

"I guess not Sam. And thanks for turning up with the cavalry."

"Yeah, but you cut it a bit fine. I got your message but not till quite a few minutes after you'd left it. Supposing I hadn't listened to my messages till later in the day? You'd be dead."

"Well, I'm not thanks to you. And you heard everything?"

"No, not everything, just the last part. We heard Kellerman saying to his wife something about 'no, put it away', then you saying something about 'you're going to shoot me Mrs. Kellerman' I assume that was for my benefit?"

"It was, well mine really. I needed you to get

in there ASAP. Thank the Lord for cell phones," said Frankie.

"Amen to that," Randazzo replied. They were both quiet for a few beats, then Randazzo said.

"Makes you think though, I mean the silencer in particular, she must have had concerns for a while about their little scheme being rumbled?"

"Not so little Sam."

"Okay, so explain to me again what happened in there just now. I mean if you're up to it. We can leave it till later if you prefer?"

"No, I'm okay Sam, keep my mind off the pain."

"Okay, if you're sure Frankie. So, what was it you said to get yourself shot in there? Oh, just before I left, that German detective Becker called, saying you'd sent him an email, but he couldn't get hold of you. Said to tell you he had some very interesting information for you, some developments. Wants you to call him when you can."

"Sounds intriguing, I'll do that."

"So, this email to Becker, what was in it?"

"Well, I thought I'd figured out what Otto was up to, so I emailed Becker to tell him about my suspicions and suggested he interrogate the photographer they'd previously arrested. Tell him they knew what the scam was. I thought if they could break him, they'd have all the proof they needed. But then I thought he might deny it, the photographer Muller I mean."

"Anyway, I decided to go and put it to Otto, see what his reaction was. The last thing I thought would happen was for me to get shot. I just didn't reckon on Hildegard. Like they say, the female of the species is always the most dangerous."

"You crazy bastard Frankie. So come on, tell me, what d'you think this Kellerman guy was up to?" Just then the ambulance slowed to a crawl. A voice came from the front of the ambulance.

"Sorry folks, traffic snarl up, how we doin' back there?" The medic sitting on the other side of the stretcher to the detective, looked at Frankie.

"You feelin' okay buddy?" Frankie said he felt okay apart from the obvious. The medic checked his vital signs once more, looked at a screen monitor, then replied to the driver.

"We're all good here, patient stable. No immediate issues."

"Understood," said the driver, "should be out of this in a couple of minutes and on our way." Frankie turned his head back to Randazzo,

"Okay, this is all supposition," he said, "but my guess is it's substantially true. Otto was selling fakes. I recalled seeing a program years ago by an Australian investigator looking into fakes produced by Chinese painters. These were not your average fakes. The paintings they produced were good enough to fool some top experts. I think Otto worked out how to take things a bit further. I think Otto Kellerman had access to many uniquely valuable works of art, plundered by the Nazis. His father being one of the leading people involved in the looting of many valuable artifacts."

"Otto was no doubt frustrated. He had access but felt unable to sell any of this illicit treasure trove, mainly because the risk of discovery should he try to move them from their secure hiding place. Then he thought about copying them, making fakes. If he could make really good fakes, virtually indistinguishable from the originals, he had it made. Added to which, the fact that he had the originals hidden away, made it unlikely in the extreme that the original would ever emerge to cause doubt about the fakes."

"Kellerman either knew Günter Müller before or somehow found him. He was a photographer who took on all manner of assignments, including art photography, but he was initially trained as a technical photographer. I looked it up and found that these photographers use modified digital cameras that take many extremely detailed images of a subject, a painting for instance. I thought, each image could provide just a bit of information of a small portion of a painting in the most detailed way. So even the tiniest brush strokes could be recorded and, with the right expertise, be re-produced in incredible detail."

"Otto presumably took Muller to where the

paintings are hidden, some Swiss bank vault, or wherever they're stashed. And he then took lots of photographs, which were then taken by Otto to China where he paid top dollar for the very best Chinese artists to faithfully recreate the paintings in incredible detail."

"What about carbon dating and all the sort of stuff. Would they pass that kind of scrutiny?" asked Randazzo.

"I don't know. But I do know the Chinese can also age the paints they use to replicate the types used by artists in the past. It all gets a bit beyond me, but essentially, I think that's what he was up to."

"So, who do you think he was selling these to?"

"Lots of incredibly wealthy collectors of unique works of 'art'," said Frankie exaggerating the word art. But more important perhaps, is where he was selling the stuff. The obvious place was via his art gallery in New York, where he no doubt arranged some very private showings. I imagine he would invite certain well vetted potential buyers and suggest they bring an expert along to verify what was on offer."

"What about the fact that they were stolen, wouldn't that limit their value?"

"On the contrary, for some collectors it may well have even added value to the paintings in question. To believe, that the paintings they purchased were part of the trove of paintings purloined by the Nazis in World War Two. That sort of notoriety may have added a certain cache for some collectors, who knows?"

"Yes, I think I can see that," said Randazzo as the ambulance began to move off again. "And I guess, shipping paintings from China directly to the USA wouldn't be that risky."

"Exactly," replied Frankie.

"So, where's the money. Presumably these paintings would command big bucks, so where's the cash hidden. Presumably he doesn't declare it.?"

"He might disguise some of it in sales of other legitimate paintings? Be a clever way to launder the cash, or at least part of it. But I think I might know how he hides the money. As you know, from gossip I heard around the pool, Otto and Hildegard are inveterate cruisers, or should I say were? Maybe buyers paid their money into an offshore bank account or accounts, say in the BVI or Grand Cayman, somewhere discreet. Probably suit both parties. Lots of illegitimate cash around."

"You saying he went on cruises to what? Collect cash from such a bank account?"

"Or accounts? Maybe he has several? My guess is that there wouldn't be much in the way of scrutiny at say Miami or Fort Lauderdale for passengers disembarking from a little Caribbean cruise?"

"You're right Frankie, there wouldn't. Perhaps more scrutiny on the way out, but coming back into the USA, probably not so much. I'm impressed Frankie, how the hell did you work all that out?"

"It was the photographer. I kept thinking about how they found no pictures of paintings, yet he was on Kellerman's books. When I found out Muller was trained in 'technical photography', I began to wonder. Then there were the trips to China, ostensibly to buy picture frames. The jigsaw started to assemble itself in my mind, but I still wasn't sure… not until Mrs. Kellerman shot me of course." They both laughed, Frankie's laugh interspersed with cries of pain.

They finally arrived at the hospital.

CHAPTER 35

PRESENT

Saturday 7 March
Frankie leaves hospital

Frankie was allowed out of hospital the following morning. He'd called Randazzo to ask if he'd pick him up. A couple of hours later the detective arrived. Frankie eased into the passenger seat of Randazzo's car with a little help from the detective and the nurse who'd been looking after him. She waved him off then went back inside.

"Thanks for picking me up Sam," said Frankie once the detective had navigated out of the hospital car park. Is our friend Otto saying anything?"

"Not initially. He screamed for a lawyer as soon as we got him to the station. Then I interviewed him and put your theory to him about what he'd been up to, and I think he knows the game's up. I said we'd be putting all his activities under scrutiny and there was no doubt we'd be able to piece it all together."

"I suggested if he cooperates it might go better for him. I told him Becker wants him back in Germany. My feeling is he'll sing. Depends if the thinks he'll get a better deal over here than in Germany. I pointed out that the German's are going to be non-too pleased at him using his father's ill-gotten gains to swindle all those people out of their rightful possessions. So, I suggested he'd be better confessing to crimes in the US. At least that will give him some time for things to die down over there in Germany."

"He will have to go back to Germany surely?"

"Eventually, yes, but maybe he'd like to delay that, we'll see. Like I say, it depends if he'd prefer American justice to what he might get in Germany."

"What did he say about Hildegard?"

"He seemed surprisingly indifferent to the fate of his wife."

"No doubt hurting inside though?"

"Somehow he didn't seem as though he was." They both laughed. "Strange bird. After we'd processed him, I called your friend Detective Becker and told him about the developments. He asked me to thank you for the information you provided and to pass on his best wishes for your recovery. I got the impression he was up to something. He said your theories were very well thought out. He was sort of amused, though I don't know why. Why would he be amused?"

"A German sense of humor. It's no laughing matter, as a friend of mine used to say." Randazzo chortled.

"That's wicked," he said and carried on laughing. He stopped and they drove along in silence for a while, then Frankie asked,

"Any update on Brandon?"

"I do," said Randazzo as he navigated through a six-lane junction. "Not good news I'm afraid though. We only heard yesterday. Brandon was killed in some kind of sting."

"Brandon dead?"

"Fraid so. Apparently, he convinced the detective, Mitchell, that he could get the killer to admit to killing his wife. So, they wired him up and arranged a meet with this alleged killer. But then instead of trying to get the guy to implicate himself, Mellor pulled out a gun and shot the alleged perp. A sniper the perp had brought along, hidden in some trees, then shot and killed Mellor. Mitchell reckons Mellor planned it all on the way back home. Says he thinks he really did love his wife and didn't care about living any more, not without her. But he was determined to kill the guy who murdered her."

"Said it looked like a combination of revenge and suicide. Reckoned he saw a smile on Brando's face when he got shot." Frankie said nothing. Randazzo looked at him. "You okay?"

"Yeah, I'm okay," Frankie said. "Just trying

to take all that in. Poor guy." After a few minutes he said. "Tell me to mind my own business Sam, but did you think any more about PTS?" Sam turned, sighed and looked at Frankie briefly before turning back to look back at the road.

"Yeah, I did. At first I thought you were a pussy for suggesting that PTS stuff. You know, us tough guys, we don't like admitting we have any weaknesses, do we?" Frankie said nothing. "After a while I thought maybe you were right," Randazzo continued, "so I did some research. It wasn't the booze so much. I can handle that. But even so, daytime drinking ain't good. So I stopped that. But then I realized it wasn't the booze, it was the pain killers. I was hooked on 'em Frankie. Me of all people, Lieutenant Detective Sam Randazzo hooked on fucking painkillers!"

"Did you know Frankie, some 50,000 died in the US last year from opioid overdoses? Some illicit use, but a lot of the stuff prescribed by doctors. Those are fucking epidemic numbers Frankie."

"No, I didn't know it was that bad," said Frankie.

"And what makes it worse is, there's people making billions from this. I don't mean dope gangs, I mean legit businesses. You know the Sackler family are one of the wealthiest families in the US, and where did they make all that money? OxyContin. I read somewhere they're worth about 60 billion dollars, 60 billion Frankie!" Frankie shook his head in disbelief. "Anyway, after you'd said what you said, I got to thinking. I haven't told anyone else this, but my marriage was going to shit. And I could tell it was starting to affect my judgment on the job." Frankie noticed Sam was gripping the steering wheel like he was going to rip it out of the dashboard.

"You hid it well."

"Yeah, I'm good at that."

"So, what did you do?"

"I sat down with Martha and talked about it. It wasn't easy. I hadn't realized how much I'd fucked things up at home. Falling asleep all the time, losing my temper, getting angry at the smallest thing, neglecting her. Generally being a major pain in the ass. So, I went cold turkey. Not so bad during the day, when I had the job to distract me, but at night… man it was tough at first, but Martha helped and after a few days I started to feel a bit better. The pain in my leg was still bad, still is, but I think trying to stop it with painkillers was doing a lot more damage. I still have a drink, but only in the evenings. I can handle that."

Frankie thought it best not to comment further and they drove along in silence for a while, then Frankie spoke.

"On another subject Sam, I had plenty of time to think about the jewels while I was in the hospital. Once I woke up from the sedatives that is."

"Shouldn't you be taking some rest from thinking? We can leave all the that for another day" Randazzo said as they turned on to the 41.

"No, I feel okay Sam. A bit sore but nothing that won't heal. Said to keep my arm in this sling for a while and they've given me some strong pain killers... oops." They both laughed.

"You were lucky," said Randazzo, "she used a .22 target pistol, with a silencer. The bullet went straight through your shoulder. If she'd used a bigger caliber gun, or aimed a few inches to the right, you'd be lying in the morgue now next to Hildegard."

"Comforting thought Sam, thanks for that."

"All I'm saying is..."

"Yeah, I know, just kidding Detective." They arrived at Acadiana. Randazzo helped Frankie out of the car.

"Give me your keys Frankie and I'll get the door for you." Frankie hobbled up the stairs to the second-floor corridor then along to his front door. Randazzo started to open the door for him.

"Hey, what about your little pooch Charlie?"

"Daisy has him. I managed to call her from the hospital and tell her what happened, so she went to get him and she's looking after him for the moment."

"Was that the first she knew about you getting shot?"

"It was, and I got my ear chewed off. Said I

must have been crazy to go and confront the guy without you being there or having some sort of backup."

"She has a point, Frankie. You're what might be called, a bit headstrong."

"That's not quite the term my business partner Barnsie used when I told him," said Frankie laughing then wincing. Randazzo smiled.

"Oh, by the way, have you heard the news?"

"What news," said Frankie.

"The US government have slapped a ban on travel to and from Europe. This virus thing. You're stuck here now."

"Right... well, if I'm going to be stuck anywhere Sam, it would be right here in Naples," he replied and went into his condo.

CHAPTER 36

Saturday 7 March 2020
SoHo New York

SoHo is situated in Manhattan. The name SoHo is an acronym for South of Houston Street, a trendy shopping area known for its elegant cast-iron-facades and cobblestone streets. The neighborhood is also an atmospheric backdrop for the fashionable set visiting high-end restaurants and nightlife hotspots. It has more than its fair share of fancy chain stores, designer boutiques and high-end art galleries.

Otto fell in love with SoHo as soon as he saw it and figured it was an ideal place for his gallery. For various reasons, one being he was not a US resident, he decided it would be easier to buy his way into an established gallery. He knew a couple of the SoHo gallery owners already, having sold them some paintings of the artists he represented. Money wasn't an issue, and he soon became the joint owner of The Cosmopolitan Art Gallery.

Jürgen and Klaus were part of the special unit within the German Federal Criminal Police Department, dedicated to tracking down the trove of stolen art stolen in WW2, along with cultural items of great significance such as, ceramics, books and religious treasures, all looted by the Nazis. Much of the plundered property had already been recovered from places such as salt mines, secluded castles and secret tunnels. But much of it remained missing.

They'd arrived in the USA earlier that evening, having flown to New York on tourist visas. The true nature of the visit would have been unlikely to have been officially approved by the US authorities. Their boss Detective Karl Becker had given them specific instructions about what they were looking for. They'd gone first to their hotel to drop off their luggage, which comprised of cabin baggage and two suitcases to reinforce their tourist credentials. The clothes inside the suitcases were disposable and just for show. Anything significant they found would be shipped back to Germany in diplomatic bags.

The gallery's alarm system was child's play for Jürgen, an experienced ex-thief who'd been turned by the authorities. He was happy with the decision to join forces with the old enemy, especially as the alternative had been a couple of decades in jail. Once into the gallery proper, they examined all the likely places where illicit material could be hidden. They scoured every room and all the individual offices, the rest rooms and broom cupboard. They removed ceiling tiles and mesh cover for the air conditioning system, but nothing.

They'd examined the small kitchen, looked behind the kitchen units, moved the oven from its housing and still nothing. Now they sat at the table in the small office kitchen and considered other possibilities. Jurgen scanned the room looking for any telltale signs of a hiding place. His attention was drawn to a shallow floor to ceiling cupboard with shelves for the meagre supplies required for an office staff kitchen.

They'd already thoroughly examined it once, but he went over to it again, opened the doors moved some tins of food, jars of coffee, and boxes of cereal, then knocked on the rear wall. He turned and smiled at Klaus. Klaus went to the kitchen door, opened it and standing astride it, one leg in the room and one in the corridor, he examined the thickness of the wall, then went back to the cupboard and ran his fingers along the edges where it attached to the wall. He looked at Jurgen and raised his eyebrows. It didn't take them long to find the latch. The cupboard swung outwards like a door.

A few minutes later they were leaving the gallery with their haul. Jurgen had already called their contact at the German Embassy, who told them where to wait and said a car would be along to collect them within the half hour. Becker had told them to call him anytime, day or night, if they found anything. Klaus called Becker while they waited for the embassy car.

"We found metal tubes with painted canvases inside. We only opened one to see what we'd got. You said if they're the real deal, they might be delicate."

"Yes, leave the others unopened," Becker said, "anything else?"

"Yes, a little cache of memory sticks in a pouch and a lot of cash, dollars."

"Okay, well once you've dropped the stuff of at the Embassy, go back to your hotel have a good night's sleep and have a day off tomorrow being tourists. You've earned it, Auf Wiedersehenn."

"Auf Wiedersehenn boss."

CHAPTER 37

PRESENT

Saturday 7 March
Loose ends

Once inside his condo, Frankie went to shower off the hospital smells and to change into some new clothes. Detective Randazzo made coffee in Frankie's kitchen, then took two mugs out on to the lanai and sat looking out over the bay while he waited for Frankie to appear. *Another stunning Florida day.* Frankie emerged looking a bit more like his old self.

"That feels better," he said as he sat down and took a sip of his coffee. "Bit tricky trying to keep the dressing dry while having a shower, but I think I managed it. So, where were we?"

"You said you'd been thinking. While you were in hospital. And I think I might be able to guess what you were thinking about. I mean apart from bedding that pretty nurse who was looking after you."

"Yes, she was a bit of a distraction I have to admit. Go on."

"The Irish Crown Jewels, the thing that started all this. We're not much further forward on that, are we? And you've been thinking on that conversation we had just prior to your near fatal visit to Otto Kellerman. About Mrs. Kennedy?"

"Correct. You want to go first, or shall I?"

"You first," said the detective.

"Okay, so we now know that Brandon had the jewels in his possession, hidden in the wall cavity. The jewels were presumably handed down from Frank Mellor, nee Shackleton, to his son William Mellor, and in turn, William Mellor handed them on to his son Brandon Mellor. But vitally, we don't know where they are now."

"Don't we?" said Randazzo smiling?

"Well again, it has to be almost certain that the artisan Sean Kennedy took the jewels when he was ripping out the walls in Brandon's condo. I also think it very likely that our friend Herr Kellerman had some hidden cash taken in the aftermath of Irma and that the guy who took it was likely the same guy who took the Irish Crown Jewels from Brandon's place."

"Sean Kennedy?"

"The same."

"Want to tell me why?" asked Randazzo draining the last of his coffee.

"Mrs. Kennedy's confession. Something doesn't add up. She told you, or the sergeant or whoever, that they'd been living 'better than they should have' wasn't that the way she put it if I remember correctly?"

"You do remember correctly yes."

"Well, the pictures taken from Sean's cell phone would suggest that the jewels were intact. There were no diamonds or rubies, or any of the precious missing, were there?" Frankie asked. Randazzo grimaced.

"So, where were they getting the money to live better 'n they should?" said Randazzo. "What a dumb bastard I am."

"Well, we don't know for certain that's what happened, but I think in the circumstances, Brandon would have said if cash had been taken from his condo as well as the jewels."

"Yeah, what you say makes a lot of sense Frankie. You know, there's always been something else that niggles in the back of my mind, about Mrs. Kennedy's confession. That day at the station."

"Yeah?"

"She came in to confess. That's a certainty, but something in the way the sergeant responded to her initially. I think I saw her change her mind. Maybe if he'd showed a bit more sympathy? But he seemed instantly exasperated. Can't blame him, the number of nutjobs we get coming in to confess stuff or fantasize about something or other. I think she changed her mind on the hoof. Changed the story she was going to tell."

"You think she maybe still has the jewels? You mean they're not missing like she said? But you went to see her, and she showed you where they'd been hidden."

"She did, and at the time I believed her, but looking back now, I don't know Frankie, but there's definitely something hinky about her story."

"I think we should maybe pay Mrs. Kennedy another visit. This time unannounced."

"Now?" asked Frankie.

"Now," replied Randazzo. "If you're up to it?"

"Try and stop me," said Frankie, "let's go.

CHAPTER 38

PRESENT

Saturday 7 March
Hello Mrs. Kennedy

They drove in silence to the Kennedy residence, each deep in their own thoughts. Frankie waited in the car until the detective had established Mrs. Kennedy was at home. Randazzo pressed the doorbell and after a while, it opened. Frankie had never seen Mrs. Kennedy, so wasn't entirely sure if it was she. Detective Randazzo turned and signaled for Frankie to come. The detective then entered the house, leaving the door open. Frankie slowly got out of the car being careful not to put any undue pressure on his wound and made his way inside the house.

It was a well-furnished, spacious single-family home. All very neat and tidy. Frankie followed the sound of voices and entered a small dining room where the person he assumed was Mrs. Kennedy was sitting at the dining table opposite the detective.

"Take a seat Frankie, this is Mrs. Kennedy."

"Pleasure to make your acquaintance Mrs. Kennedy," said Frankie.

"I just love your accent Mr....?"

"Armstrong," said Frankie. "Frankie Armstrong."

"And such lovely manners," she continued. Are you with the police as well?"

"Not officially, I'm just assisting the detective here."

"Well nice to meet you, would you like a drink? I guess you drink tea, do you? All the British drink tea I'm told."

"Sometimes I do yes, but I'm okay at the moment thanks," said Frankie looking at Randazzo who was obviously wanting done with the small talk and anxious to move things along.

"Mrs. Kennedy," said Randazzo, "you don't mind if I record this conversation, do you?" The question obviously threw Mrs. Kennedy, but she said.

"Okay, if you want to, I suppose it's alright." Randazzo placed his cell on the table and started talking again.

"The last time I was here, we talked about the missing jewels you said you thought your late husband may have stolen."

"Yes, that's correct."

"When you came to the station, you said you wanted to tell us about the jewels and how you'd been living better then you should, implying that the theft of the jewels coincided with your..., how shall we say, improved lifestyle?" Mrs. Kennedy looked a bit flustered but kept herself composed.

"Yes, I did, I told you all I know so I'm not sure what it is you want with me now."

"Are the jewels still missing Mrs. Kennedy?" asked Frankie. She turned and looked at him.

"Of course they are. You think whoever took them decided to bring them back?"

"I don't think you're being entirely truthful with us Mrs. Kennedy," Randazzo said. Mrs. Kennedy straightened up in her chair and tried to look indignant.

"I beg your pardon. Are you calling me a liar?" Randazzo ignored the question and carried on talking.

"Explain to us how your improved lifestyle was being funded. Although you implied it had something to do with your husband stealing the jewels, they were intact. You said the jewels had gone missing. The jewels hadn't been sold, nor were there any of the precious stones missing in the pictures on Sean's phone. You said you'd been on expensive vacations and such. Where did the money come from to fund those vacations Mrs. Kennedy?" Mrs. Kennedy looked pale. She shook her head but said nothing.

"I think when you came to the police station that day, you weren't coming to talk about the jewels. That was part of it, but you were coming to confess about the money as well, weren't you? You wanted to make a clean breast of things. You changed your mind about confessing. You just used pieces of your story to justify coming into the station and making a report. It was on your conscience wasn't it Mrs. Kennedy? and still is. I know you're a religious woman and I think your husband's funeral was a turning point somehow, wasn't it? It reminded you that we all go to our maker in the end, and you wanted a clear conscience didn't you Mrs. Kennedy?"

Randazzo's voice had slowly increased in volume as he piled on the pressure. Frankie kept still, his mouth firmly shut. Mrs. Kennedy looked affronted, opened her mouth to speak, and then shut it again. No one said anything for a few beats, then the dam burst. It began with a wail and then morphed into violent sobbing. Frankie couldn't help feeling sorry for her. Randazzo obviously wasn't feeling any pity. He had her on the ropes and he was going in for the kill. Randazzo's next question shocked Frankie.

"How did your husband die Mrs. Kennedy. I know what it said on the autopsy report, but how did he actually die? What caused his death? Did you kill him?" Mrs. Kennedy stopped crying and looked up at the detective. She seemed incapable of speech. She just nodded her head and then recommenced wailing and sobbing. Randazzo got up and left the room briefly, then came back with a glass of water and some tissues, by which time the wailing had ceased and sobbing subsided to some quiet mewling and sniffing.

Frankie kept quiet, not wishing to interrupt the detective's flow. Randazzo put the water on the table in front of Mrs. Kennedy together with the box of tissues then sat down, folded his arms and waited. Mrs. Kennedy picked up the water with both hands, took a sip, put the glass down, then took a tissue out of the box, dabbed her eyes then blew her nose noisily. She looked up again at Randazzo.

"You want to tell us what really happened now?" She began without preamble.

"It was a Friday night. The kids had both gone out with their friends. Sean had dropped into a bar with his buddies on the way home. He was always trouble when that happened. When he got home, we got into a fight. I wanted to give back whatever money we had left, tell someone about the jewels. Anonymously I mean, I didn't say we should admit to anything, didn't want either of us to go to jail or anything. But I was sick of living a lie."

"Sean could be very vicious at times. He told me if I ever said anything he'd kill me. He wouldn't hurt a kitten when he was sober, but when he had the drink in him, he turned into a different person. The argument got really heated and he went to hit me, then I think he had some sort of seizure. He suddenly clasped his hand to his chest and collapsed on the couch in there." she pointed to the living room area on the other side of the hall. "I was angry, angrier than I'd ever been. And instead of calling 911, I left him and went upstairs and lay down on the bed."

"I must have fallen asleep. I woke up not long after and the anger had all gone. I rushed downstairs and I knew just by looking at him that he was dead. So yes, I did kill Sean detective. I killed my husband." She sobbed a small sob.

"And the money. I assume Sean had stolen money, cash?"

"Yes, he stole it. Well, he said he found it, but we both knew that was a lie. He took it from one of those condos in Roman Plaza. I told him they would come looking for him, the cops, as soon as it was reported missing. But he said it would never be reported. And he was right, no one ever came looking. We didn't spend any for a while just in case."

"He found the jewels in one of the condos, hidden in the cavity in the wall. He found the cash in another condo. He said it was a metal box in a locked cupboard, but that wouldn't stop Sean. I told him again that he'd be in trouble when they reported the money missing. But Sean laughed and said it would never be reported. Said he could smell funny money a mile away, and this was definitely funny money. He said there'd be no good reason to hide that amount of legit money in a condo. There's quite a bit of the cash left. I don't know how much there was to begin with, but there's still a lot left."

"Please show us Mrs. Kennedy," said the detective.

"Follow me," she said." They all got up and followed Mrs. Kennedy upstairs and into a bedroom. She opened a closet. There were clothes hanging there.

"These are Sean's. I couldn't throw them away, I don't know why. He's not coming back, is he?" Frankie wasn't sure if she was making a dark joke, but from the look on her face, she obviously hadn't spoken in jest. She pointed to a soft luggage bag on a shelf above the clothes. "It hasn't been moved since Sean died. It's a bit too heavy for me to get down."

"May I use that chair to stand on?" Randazzo asked. Mrs. Kennedy didn't answer, just nodded. The detective took down the bag and placed it on the bed. It wasn't locked and Randazzo unzipped it. It was full of cash. Dollars in large denominations.

"Any idea how much is in there?" asked Frankie.

"A lot," said Randazzo. "Rough guess, more than a couple a hundred grand and less than a million." Frankie raised his eyebrows.

"Okay," said Randazzo, "now the jewels, where are they hidden now?"

"Oh, I got rid of those," said Mrs. Kennedy.

"I thought if someone found them, I don't know, but I thought... I don't know what I thought, but I thought if I get caught with those, then somehow it would be worse than the money. I thought I might be able to explain the money. Say that Sean had won it, I don't know, but those jewels I could never explain those away, could I? So, I got rid of them."

"How exactly did you get rid of them?" said Randazzo obviously finding it hard to remain calm.

"I took them to the consignment shop, the one on the 41, next to that garage where they sell all those fancy upmarket cars. Sean used to take me there to look at the cars, but I told him, if he bought one of those, the cops would find out for certain that he more money than he could explain."

"When did you take the jewels to the consignment store Mrs. Kennedy?"

"Just after I'd been to the police station detective, before you came to see me."

"Do you have a ticket or anything?"

"No. I didn't want the jewels to be connected to me, so I gave them a false name and address. I threw the ticket away." The detective looked at Frankie his face etched with disbelief.

"Just out of interest, did they say how much it might sell for Mrs. Kennedy?" asked Frankie.

"I told them it was fake costume jewelry and they said they might bring a couple of hundred dollars if I was lucky." Frankie looked at Randazzo who was standing with one hand rubbing his forehead looking down at the floor. He seemed to be in a trance, then he looked up, checked his watch and said,

"Right, all get in my car now!"

"I can't leave the house now. My friend is coming round to see me."

"I said get in the car now toots" barked Randazzo, "or I'll slap some handcuffs on you and frog march you out of your house in front of all your neighbors."

"Toots?" said Frankie to Randazzo as the woman obeyed. The detective shrugged his shoulders.

"Sometimes you just have to be assertive," he said smiling. Then the detective took Mrs. Kennedy firmly by the arm and they walked down the path to his car. He opened the rear door, helped her into the back, then went and helped Frankie into the front passenger seat. He went round the driver's side, about to get in then stopped.

"Shit," he said, "forgot the bag." Frankie laughed. Randazzo went back, in the house, retrieved the bag, came back out, put the bag in the trunk, then got in and drove at speed to the junction of the 41. He turned right and drove north towards the garage that sold Porsches, Bentleys and Roll Royce's and all other manner of expensive cars. Frankie remembered the consignment shop Mrs. Kennedy was talking about. It was located in a small mall on the next block to the garage. They drove into the mall and parked. Randazzo jumped out and helped Mrs. Kennedy out of the back of the car and walked her quickly towards the consignment store.

Frankie exited the passenger seat as quickly as he could and followed on. By the time he got into the store, Randazzo was talking to a stern looking lady wearing glasses on a gold chain around her neck. Frankie heard her reply as he got nearer.

"I can't recall this lady I'm afraid, nor the piece of jewelry you describe, but we put all our costume jewelry in one of two cabinets. I'll show you. You're a policeman you say?" Randazzo said he was and reached in his pocket for his badge and ID. "Very well," she said "follow me please. They reached on cabinet and looked at the display, nothing resembling the Irish Crown Jewels was there. "No, nothing here you recognize?" Randazzo shook his head, "well let's try the other one," and they all trooped behind her to the next room and another display cabinet.

"No, nothing here either," said Randazzo, his face looking grim. He looked at Frankie with an expression of resignation on his face. "Shit!" he said loudly. The lady from the store looked at him disapprovingly. "Sorry about that ma'am. Come on, let's go," the detective said to Frankie and Mrs. Kennedy. As they walked towards the door, the store lady said.

"There is one more place we could look. If it doesn't look as though it will sell quickly, we sometimes store the tackier stuff in the back room, keep the display space free for stuff we think will move quickly. We can try looking in the back if you like?"

"Why not?" said Randazzo, looking defeated. They trudged into the back room. It was full of furniture with dust sheets thrown over, some broken furniture, a shelf with glasses and pottery on. Some very strange looking paintings on the wall and various bit of bric-a-brac strewn around the floor. The lady went to a cabinet and pulled out a large drawer. It was full of various bits of cheap costume jewelry. The sunlight streaming through a high window shone on the dusty miscellany of necklaces, bangles and brooches.

One particular stone glinted with exceptional brightness. Randazzo gently pulled out the whole piece and held it up to the light. It was the smaller one of the two precious items they were looking for. He rummaged amongst the other jewelry in the drawer and uncovered the larger piece. It was covered in dust but there was no mistaking it. The detective held both pieces in his hands, looked at Frankie and shook his head slightly Frankie got the message, *keep shtum.*

Mrs. Kennedy was about to speak when Frankie took her arm and said,

"Let's us go and wait for the detective outside, shall we?" And he gently propelled Mrs. Kennedy out of the store and into the car park. Randazzo came out some time later looking very pleased with himself.

"Did you explain?" asked Frankie smiling, knowing what the response would be.

"No, I thought that might get too complicated. I offered her $150 for both pieces and she snatched my hand off, seemed delighted." The detective carefully placed the jewels in the trunk of his car then opened the rear door and motioned for Mrs. Kennedy to get in.

"What happens to me now?" she asked the detective in a plaintive voice.

"I'm afraid I'm going to take you down to the station Mrs. Kennedy, where you'll be asked to provide a formal statement and I guess you'll be charged with various offences. I can't figure out what those might be, I'm gonna let someone else figure out precisely what you'll be charged with. You got a lawyer?" She shook her head. "Okay well they'll get one for you. I suggest you don't answer any questions until you have a lawyer present, but I didn't tell you that, okay?"

"Oh..., oh, yes, I think so, thanks detective. But what about my kids, they'll be expecting me to be there when they get home."

"You got a friend or neighbor you can call to deal with that for now?"

"Yes, I'll call my friend Joyce, she has a key

to the house. But what am I going to tell her?" she asked, her voice faltering as she asked the question.

"I'll leave you to figure that one out, now please get in Mrs. Kennedy, let's go." She got in and Frankie got into the front passenger seat. Randazzo dropped Frankie at Acadiana. Frankie got out of the car, the detective got out as well and closed the car door. He looked at Frankie.

"What?" said Frankie. Randazzo nodded his head in the direction of Mrs. Kennedy sitting in the car huddled up and looking forlorn.

"What good is it going to do, her being prosecuted an all? I mean, she has two kids, what's going to happen to them?"

"You going soft Sam?"

"Maybe, but what has she actually done? I know she told us she killed Sean, but she didn't, did she? He'd been drinking, had a heart attack. He was probably dead as soon as he collapsed. Who's to say now if the medics would have got there in time to save him? I mean, she didn't actually kill him, did she? Anyway, any halfway decent lawyer would get her off on that one easy. So why put her through the trauma? She's suffered enough, look at her."

"What about the jewels, and the money?"

"Yeah, there's that. But what are we gonna charge her with? She didn't steal anything did she. It was her asshole of a husband. She's as honest as the day's long. She came to the station to confess for God's sake!"

"So, what are you going to do?"

"I don't know. I'm gonna have a quiet word with the captain, see what he thinks." Randazzo shook his head and got back in the car and rolled down the window. "I'll call you, let you know developments," said Randazzo and drove off, taking the wretched miserable Mrs. Kennedy to face the music..., or possibly not.

CHAPTER 39

PRESENT

Monday 9 March Late afternoon
The luck of the Irish

Frankie was out walking Charlie when Randazzo called his cell.

"Where are you?" asked Randazzo. Frankie told him. "You want to speak now, or call me when you get back to your condo?"

"If it's about the jewels, I'll call you back if that's okay?"

"It is."

"Okay, call you in about ten minutes." Frankie got back to his condo, made a coffee then took it to the lanai, sat down and called the detective. Randazzo answered on the third ring.

"So come on, what news?"

"Okay Frankie, well I spent this morning telling the whole story about the jewels to Chief O'Sullivan and got seriously upbraided for keeping it to myself for all this time. Chewed me out for a good ten minutes. But he eventually calmed down and then we had a discussion about the next moves. And by the way, he wants to meet you to thank you personally. Says paying you for your time won't be a problem."

"Okay, thanks," said Frankie, "what about Mrs. Kennedy?"

"Went better than I thought. I explained everything to O'Sullivan, then the Chief, he spoke with her in private. He was in there a while, then came out we had another little discussion."

"So?"

"So, the Chief doesn't know what to make of things either. The whole situation is such a fuck up. But when you get down to it… I mean, the Germans are almost certainly going to get their man Otto back. They say they've found enough to charge him with something serious, and they reckon there's plenty more to uncover. So, we're not gonna get involved in that, other than telling all we know."

"Mrs. Kellerman, well she's dead, so that's her done. Brandon Mellor, poor sap. He did what he had to do and chose well in my opinion. Took another asshole off the face of the earth and paid for it with his life. I only hope he's happily back up there with his wife, who he obviously couldn't live without."

"Wow, you have got a heart Sam, who would have believed?"

"Yeah, well you just don't tell anyone else,

or I'll kill you, okay?" Frankie laughed.

"Okay Sam, your secret's safe with me. So, what about those Crown Jewels?"

"Well, we looked at the options for informing the Irish authorities. At first, we thought the Irish police, the Garda in Dublin. But then we decided we should talk to the Irish Consulate's office in New York first. Once we'd convinced the people there this wasn't some sort of elaborate hoax, the Irish Ambassador himself came on the phone, guy called T.E. Dermot Mulhall. He asked a lot of questions and told us he'd call us back. About an hour later he called and said that both the Irish President and the Taoiseach had gotten involved, and the upshot is, he's flying down here this afternoon to have a look for himself."

"Did he say anything else?"

"I didn't talk to him directly. Chief O'Sullivan spoke with him, but I was in the room. The Chief says his impression was, they're excited but skeptical."

"I can understand that. He'll want to take them back with him, won't he?"

"That's what the Chief thinks, yeah."

"Will the Chief let him?"

"We talked about that too, and I think he's inclined to let them go. I mean, what would we do with them? Brandon Mellor who had them and hid them is dead. Kennedy, the guy who stole them from where Mellor hid them is dead. Looks like we're gonna let things slide with Mrs. Kennedy. It seems the rightful owners are the Irish government, whatever. I assume there's no Irish Royal Family now?" Frankie laughed.

"Not that I'm aware of," he said.

"Thought not."

"Well Sam, thanks for letting me know. I'll be fascinated to hear what happens next."

"I'll keep you posted Frankie," replied the detective.

CHAPTER 40

PRESENT

Frankie & Son

When it was all over, Frankie returned to the matter of Aaron, the son he didn't know existed before a couple of weeks ago. He'd emailed Aaron to ask what dates he might be free to come and spend a couple of days with Frankie, so they could get to know each other. Aaron had replied and now Frankie was sitting in his rental car outside arrivals at Fort Myers airport.

He spotted Aaron as he emerged through the doors and got out to wave. Aaron was tall and athletic looking. They man hugged briefly and Frankie opened the door for Aaron. As they drove along, Frankie asked Aaron to tell him a bit about his life, his adopted family, his friends at college and his interests and hobbies. Aaron chatted away happily telling Frankie all about himself and gladly answered any questions Frankie asked.

Frankie was particularly pleased to find that fishing was amongst Aaron's interests.

"Well, I'd been wondering how we might spend our time together, so now we have a shared interest in fishing, I'll arrange to hire a boat for a few days, and we can go out fishing in the Gulf anytime you like."

"I'd like that," said Aaron and began to tell Frankie tales of his various catches and the inevitable stories about the ones that got away. Once they were back at the condo, Frankie showed Aaron his bedroom and went to sit at his PC leaving Aaron to freshen up after his journey. Aaron appeared a while later and Frankie gave him a brief tour of the condo.

"Just make yourself at home, take anything you want, apart from the booze." Aaron smiled. Frankie looked at his watch. "Look it's five thirty now, so what says we have a coffee on the lanai, or maybe you prefer a soda?" Aaron plumped for a coke and Frankie got himself a beer. "If you're hungry, we can go to Pepe's Pizza and grab a pizza or some pasta, steak whatever?"

"Sounds good to me Frankie."

They sat on the lanai looking out over the swimming pool and Venetian Bay. Frankie pointed out the boat docks that lined the sea wall just beyond the swimming pool and told Aaron the story of the shark that attacked a woman who'd been pushed into the bay. Frankie went and got a couple more drinks and they continued chatting, then Aaron said.

"So, I, er, I wondered if you would ask for a DNA test?"

"Why do you say that?" asked Frankie taking a sip of his beer.

"I suppose I wanted to get it out of the way."

"Not necessary. But I can appreciate why you want to raise it and get it out of the way. I think I'd do the same thing, not have it hanging over me. Might as well see if that's what I'm going to do at some point?"

"So, you believe me regardless." Frankie hesitated before replying.

"Let's just say, I believe your motives for wanting me as a father are not bad motives.

"I don't understand," said Aaron.

"I haven't asked for a DNA test because I knew the result would be negative. It would confirm I'm not your biological father."

Aaron looked shocked. He gulped a couple of times then spoke.

"I thought.... "I thought maybe..., no, I hoped maybe you wouldn't. I thought somehow it would just be better if you believed me. I took a chance, but you're right, I had to bring it up, because I thought you might in the future and then..."

"Yeah, I get it."

"So why, I mean how can you be so certain?"

"First, the reason I knew any test would come back negative is because I'm infertile. I was tested some years ago. The doctor told me I'd probably always been infertile.

"Oh." Aaron grimaced.

"And second, you want to know why I invited you and why I've carried on the pretense?" Aaron nodded sheepishly. "Well, you clearly knew Hana and I do believe you read her diary. As for the rest…? So do you want to tell me your story again, and this time no lies okay?" Aaron drew in a big breath, breathed out, looked at the view of the bay, took a sip of his coke, then said.

"Okay. Well, we are sort of related, but not in the way I said. My mother is Naza, Hana's sister. I'm sorry. I lied about when Hana died. She was killed as you'd thought, when the hospital was bombed." Frankie took a long swig of beer.

"Carry on," he said.

"You know what it was like in Iraq for us Christians. We were isolated and disliked by most other Iraqis. My mother said in many ways, we had more in common with the American and British soldiers than with many of our own countrymen." Frankie nodded. "Anyway, my mother Naza, also fell for a British soldier and became pregnant with me. When she told him, he told her he was already married and would be going back to his wife in the UK, but that he would send her money. She said she refused at first and told him to go away and leave her alone, but then decided if he wasn't going to marry her and take her back to the UK, then at least he should pay something towards my upkeep."

"Things were hard she said, and she wouldn't be able to work and look after a child as well. So, a few days later, she contacted the army in Basra and got in touch with the commander of his regiment. He checked and told her that the soldier she was enquiring about had been killed the previous day. So, you see, their story was very similar to Hana and yours, but the other way round. My mother survived the war, but my father didn't. That's it."

"I'm sorry I lied Frankie, but I wanted a father. I read Hana's diary and she wrote about what a really wonderful person you were, so I thought, well I thought.... I don't really know what I thought. I'm sorry. I'll call the airline and see if I can get a flight back as soon as possible."

"Not so fast young man," said Frankie, "I was looking forward to a couple of days fishing. Won't be much fun on my own."

"You serious?" said Aaron.

"Yeah, I am. Look Aaron, life's a bitch. Sometimes things happen for a reason. Sometimes it's best not to ask too many questions. Just accept good fortune when it comes knocking."

"How do you mean, good fortune?"

"Well Aaron, I always wanted a son, and you want a father. You actually wanted me as a father, and I'm flattered. Not sure if I'll live up to your expectations, nor you to mine. But I'm willing to give it a chance if you are."

CHAPTER 41

PRESENT

Tuesday 17 March
When Irish eyes are smiling

Aaron had gone back home after spending a couple of days with Frankie. They'd been fishing, gone on trips to the Everglades, and sometimes just walked Charlie around Naples so Aaron could get acquainted with the local geography. Aaron and Frankie had got on well together. Frankie had introduced Aaron to Daisy, and they too seemed to like each other. By mutual unspoken agreement, the subject of son and father hadn't been discussed again. Frankie didn't refer to Aaron as son, and Aaron didn't refer to Frankie as dad, or pop.

They'd agreed that Aaron would come back down to visit Frankie again as soon as time and college permitted. Saying goodbye at the airport had been a bit awkward to begin with. They shook hands in a manly fashion, but then Aaron stood back then forward and hugged Frankie and thanked him for a great couple of days. Frankie told him the feeling was mutual. Aaron smiled, turned and walked away.

After Aaron had left, Frankie felt the void in his life more than ever. but consoled himself that he now had something tangible out of his relationship with Hana. He busied himself with business matters, spent a bit more time at the boxing gym, hung out with some of the guys from the gym at one of the local sports bars and occasionally hired a boat to go out fishing in the Gulf, or went fishing off Naples pier, or chewed the fat with the other Acadiana residents around the pool.

The news media had got hold of the story, but Frankie had refused to talk to them until Daisy had had the chance to make a big splash about it herself, and in particular, her inside knowledge and involvement. Frankie was a bit embarrassed at first at being the focus of so much attention at Acadiana. He was constantly asked to repeat the story about Otto Kellerman and Brandon Mellor. It was a bit of a drag, but he understood and gave the other residents as much information as he felt he could.

The locals were thrilled to have such dramatic events happening at the otherwise sleepy and peaceful Moorings. Frankie was inundated with dinner invitations, most of which he declined. The interest gradually waned as more dramatic stories hit the headlines, one particularly gruesome one of several mutilated bodies found hidden in the everglades.

About a week after he'd last spoken to Detective Randazzo, the detective called as he was sunbathing by the pool.

"You okay to speak Frankie?"

"Depends, I'm just by the pool soaking up the sun."

"Up to you, but you might want to go to your apartment and sit down for this."

"Uh oh, bad news?"

"Not bad, no, well… listen go back to your place, get comfortable and call me, okay?" Frankie did as the defective suggested, had a quick shower, then looked at his watch. Five o'clock. *Not too early for a beer..* He got a Rolling Rock out of the fridge, went to the lanai, sat down, had a swig of beer, put the bottle down on the coffee table and called the detective.

"Sat down and ready Sam," he said when the detective answered the phone.

"Well, first Otto Kellerman. Detective Becker wants him back in Germany."

"Oh, I thought you implied Kellerman might want to take his chances over here."

"Well, he might have wanted to, but to begin with, he's not a US citizen and like I said Becker says he's got some pretty incriminating stuff on him."

"Any idea what that is?"

"He says you steered him in the right direction and that led to them finding certain items hidden in his New York Art Gallery. Fake paintings and photographs of what they assume are original stolen works of art."

"So, I was right."

"Seems so, you smartass sonovabitch. Says he has enough for an extradition warrant. He also says they've used the information they've now got, to sweat the photographer, and they think they might know where the genuine stolen paintings are hidden. Becker says this could be huge, and a lot of it is down to you. Says we'll be reading about it soon enough. He wants you to call him sometime. No rush he says, anytime."

"Okay, I look forward to that conversation. Might get a trip to Germany out of it?"

"I'm guessing you will Frankie. Oh, by the way, news on Sarah Kennedy. It looks like Mrs. Kennedy is going to skate."

"Really, how so?"

"It's complicated, but basically, we don't really have much to charge her with. Wasting police time maybe, but not much more."

"But what about the jewels?"

"Well, like I said to you before, she didn't steal 'em did she? She wasn't complicit in stealing them, so.... And the death of her husband, no one wants to go there. It would be virtually impossible to prove she had any hand in that, even if she did fail to call the emergency services when she should have. There were no witnesses to the event, other than her, so…"

"What about the stolen money?" asked Frankie still trying to digest what he'd already been told.

"Well, you're not gonna believe this."

"Try me, said Frankie, "I think I can guess what's coming."

"She's not going to be charged with anything relating to that either." Frankie didn't speak. "You still there Frankie?"

"Yeah, still here, just speechless. Come on, how so?"

"Think about it. We don't know where that money came from, do we? If you remember, when she first showed it to us, she said Sean told her he'd found it."

"Yes, but then she went on to say that she and Sean both knew that was a lie, didn't she?"

"She did, but that's not proof, is it? You and I may feel certain Sean stole it from Otto's condo. But Sean is dead, so we can't ask him. And Otto is hardly going to claim he's had some of his fraudulent stash of money stolen, is he?"

"I guess not. So, what happens to the money… don't tell me… she gets to keep it!"

"She does. Theoretically, I suppose the tax authorities might have a claim on some of it, if they find out about it that is. But, other than that, yeah, she gets to keep it." Frankie was silent again. "Like I've said before, it's a funny old world Frankie boy," said the detective.

"And the Crown Jewels?"

"Yeah, the Crown Jewels, right. Well, the Irish Ambassador called us a couple of hours ago and told us that they had experts poring over the jewels for a couple of days. Initially," he said, "there was some disagreement as to their authenticity. Some experts said they were definitely genuine others disagreed, but eventually, after some further extensive tests, they were able to say that the jewels are definitely fake."

"What?!" said Frankie knocking his bottle of beer over. "Shit," said Frankie, "just knocked something over. Give me a minute." Sam laughed. Frankie put the phone down, wiped up the mess and picked the phone up again. "So, after all that they're fake?"

"Well, yes and no."

"Come on Sam, either they're fake or not, surely?"

"It's not quite as simple as that. See, they're very good fakes and in some respects genuine."

"I don't understand."

"The metal the forger, or whatever a faker of jewelry is called, used, is real gold. Eighteen carats apparently. They say the detail is astonishing. And conclude that the forger must have had the original jewels in his possession to work from."

"What about the gemstones?"

"Well, this is where it gets really interesting. Apparently, during the 1800s, people had already developed certain techniques and discovered how to produce very convincing replicas of precious stones. The process became much more refined by the beginning of the 1900s. They say that there were some real diamonds used for the replica jewels, but false ones as well. The other gemstones used, rubies and sapphires and so on, were all extremely realistic fakes."

"So, what would be the point of going to all that trouble?" Frankie asked. Randazzo didn't reply. "Hang on, I've just got it. Christ on a bike!"

"Took me a while as well," said the detective.

"Someone somehow borrowed the real crown jewels, so the forger could make a convincing replica. Then they switched the replica for the genuine ones. Then along came Frank Shackleton who stole what he believed were the genuine crown jewels."

"You got it. The real ones were stolen earlier. How much earlier is anyone's guess."

"So, the real crown jewels are still missing? I wonder who stole the real ones, and what they're worth today?"

"The Irish Ambassador says, they'll probably never know who stole them. I asked him about the likely value, and he said it's hard to say, but many millions of dollars. But then, maybe the crown jewels were broken up and sold off piecemeal?"

"So, this whole thing has been a bit of a pointless exercise, a complete waste of time and effort, a wild goose chase? And... bang goes the prospect of a reward."

"Not quite Frankie. This will kill you. The Irish think the fake Crown Jewels are a real find."

"How so?"

"Even though they're fake, you're going to get a reward anyway. Probably a big one I think."

"What about you?"

"Serving police officer, I'm not allowed to receive rewards. All part of the job, see?"

"I see, but why any reward at all?" said Frankie.

"The ambassador says their tourist PR department are in overdrive, they think this is one hell of a story. They say it's got the lot, notoriety, daring theft, tragedy, the works. They've got the brother of the big-name famous explorer Earnest Shackleton stealing the Irish Crown Jewels, being jailed, then changing his name, passing the stolen jewels down through two generations, then tragically Brandon Mellor losing his wife in a violent death, then avenging her and getting killed in the process."

"They plan to display the fake Irish Crown Jewels in Dublin Castle. Reckon the publicity will generate millions in tourist revenue. They're convinced people will flock to see them."

"Hmm," said Frankie, "I suppose they might be right. Luck of the Irish!"

"You never know Frankie. Bruce Willis might even make a movie of it? Then you'll be in the money."

"Yeah right," Frankie laughed.

"By the way, you do know what date it is today?"

"Erm, yes I guess so, its March 17, isn't it?"

"Correct, and you know what March 17 is don't you?" Frankie took a moment, then suddenly realized. He started laughing and couldn't stop.

****

Dear Reader

I enjoyed writing this book. I hope you enjoyed reading it. I like to write a mixture of fact and fiction and being of Irish heritage myself, I particularly enjoyed writing about the theft of The Irish Crown Jewels. Sadly, the Irish Crown Jewels are still missing - or are they? Could they be gathering dust is some pawn shop or consignment store somewhere - thought of as just some tacky costume jewellery?

THANKS (and review request)

And, thanks for taking the time to read my book. I hope you enjoyed it. I love hearing from all of you and I take the time to read all the emails and reply. I also love reading your reviews. If you enjoyed this work, I'd be very grateful if you would leave a review and rate this book on Amazon. Why? Because reviews help others find my work and that in turn helps me to keep on writing. And also of course, I love knowing that someone has enjoyed my work. Bless you!

Kerry

AUTHOR'S NOTES

Fact & Fiction

This book is a mixture of fact and fiction. The theft of the Irish Crown Jewels did take place in 1907 and the main suspect was indeed Frank Shackleton, brother of the famed Antarctic explorer Sir Ernest Henry Shackleton CVO OBE FRGS FRSGS. Frank Shackleton was later convicted for fraud and spent time in jail, then moved to the south of England, having changed his name to Mellor. The letter that appears in the book, pertaining to this, is genuine.

The characters Brandon and his father are purely fictional constructs of my imagination. Likewise, the character of Otto Kellerman and Hildegard, and their respective fathers', as featured in this book, are also completely fictional, though much of the story about the Nazis plundering valuable artifacts and paintings etc., is true. The estimated value of this illicit treasure trove is claimed to be worth billions of dollars and much of it remains undiscovered.

All rights reserved ISBN 978-1-9164259-8-9

DEDICATIONS

For Joe Mainous, Capt. Dave Ramsey (Park Shore Marina) & all our dear friends at The Orleans

Acknowledgements

Lyn Costello

Edmund Pickett

Gabi Rosetti

Jasia Painter

John Sansom

ABOUT THE AUTHOR

Kerry Costello

Kerry Costello was born in England but is of Irish heritage. In his late twenties, he started his own successful travel business, eventually selling out to focus on enjoying life, traveling, fishing, cooking, and writing novels. Costello says he feels more Irish than English and is very much at home in America where he and his wife Lyn have had a home for many years.

"The Irish are great story tellers and poets," says Costello. "James Joyce, Samuel Beckett, Oscar Wilde, W B Yeats, Edna O'Brien, Brendan Behan, the list goes on. I don't claim to be in the same class as these people, but I enjoy writing and entertaining people with my stories. We have a small bay side condo in Naples Florida, where I find lots of inspiration for my crime mystery novels".

PRAISE FOR AUTHOR

"This author has a rather unique way of writing style leaning predominantly towards a narrative with shortish sentences. Yet it leans towards a no nonsense approach that is easy to follow and tends to build suspense rather easily.

- MANIE KILIAN - USA

BOOKS BY THIS AUTHOR

No Way Back

One beautiful sunny morning in May, Jack Brandon takes his dog Bess for their usual early morning walk in the Cheshire countryside, and suddenly Jack's pleasant and peaceful world turns into a violent nightmare. A chance meeting changes his life forever. Jack now has a secret or two, and is pursued by some powerful people who want answers - they'll stop at nothing to get what they're after.

The Long Game

A dramatic story fuelled by years of unresolved bitter hatred, and revenge - with a shocking twist that that will elude you until the very last page.
Police Sergeant Gibson investigates what appears to be an elderly man's death by natural causes. Using instinct, good old fashioned detective work and a dogged determination to get at the truth - Sergeant Gibson pieces together an intri-

cate puzzle of long awaited retribution.

Florida Clowns

Lorna's life depends on Gibson believing her incredible story. He knows anyone in her situation would lie. in just a few short weeks, Lorna faces execution by lethal injection.

Ex British detective Gibson returned to Florida to find work as a Private Eye, but didn't expect his first assignment to be so tough. He's tasked to rescue a fellow Brit from death row. Lorna claims she's been set up. Does Gibson believe her, or is Lorna sending him on a wild goose chase? Will Gibson find the truth out in time – and what evil might lurk behind a clown's painted smile?
Find out in this spine-chilling thriller.

You Owe Me

Mafia thugs. Sunken treasure. Can an ex-soldier solve the case before he's dragged under?
Frankie Armstrong's skills in combat never prepared him for his wife's rejection. Desperate and depressed, the former British soldier gets just the distraction he needs when the American who saved his life calls in a favor. But shortly after arriving on Florida's sun-soaked coast, a simple search and rescue mission gets tangled up with lowlifes and murderers
Joined by a loyal stray dog, Frankie races to stay a

step ahead of the police force, a rival PI, and ruthless mafia henchmen. But when he learns that his old pal left out a million-dollar detail, he fears his furry companion is the only one he can trust. But will Frankie's attempt to repay an old debt cost him his life?

You Owe Me is an edge-of-your-seat crime thriller. If you like fast-paced storytelling, high-octane chases, and twists that keep you guessing, then you'll love Kerry Costello's gripping tale.

Florida Shakedown

"An exciting read, with a terrific ending that won't disappoint"

Retired ex British detective Gibson travels to Florida to recover from a tragic family bereavement. All he wants is peace and quiet, but Jack, a resident of the holiday condo he's staying at, has other ideas. He persuades Gibson to look at the death of his business partner in bizarre and brutal circumstances. Gibson is hooked, and against his better judgement, agrees to help. He's soon drawn into a violent corrupt and terrifying world where his very own survival is at risk.

Condo

After attempting to rescue a woman attacked by a gator in an otherwise peaceful Florida condo community, ex British soldier Frankie Armstrong becomes suspicious. Was it a freak accident, or was it something more sinister?

The more he looks into the lives of his fellow condo residents, the more troubled Frankie becomes. Nothing and no one are as they seem. Using all the resources at his disposal to expose the truth, he attempts to hunt down the killer and bring him to justice... But will he succeed, or will the killer find him first?

CONDO is an edge-of-your-seat crime thriller. If you like fast-paced storytelling with twists that keep you guessing until the end, then you'll enjoy this gripping tale.

Printed in Great Britain
by Amazon